The Chosen Ones

Oglala Warriors

Dangerous Missions

in the Northwest

A Series of Campfire Story Telling

Book 2

Works by Jerry Barrett

**The Chosen Ones Oglala Warriors
A Series of Campfire Story Telling**

The Chosen Ones

Oglala Warriors

Dangerous Missions

in the Northwest

A Series of Campfire Story Telling

Book 2

FOR MIKE,
GO FOR IT!
Jerry Barrett

JERRY BARRETT

www.jerrybarrett.net

Printed in the United States of America

ISBN 978-1-7349377-1-8

Dedication

I dedicate this series of novels "The Chosen Ones Oglala Warriors" to the welfare of the Oglala Lakota Indians and all other Indigenous people, including the native Hawaiians who lost their paradise and most especially the youthful. My goal is to bring awareness of the Oglala Lakota people and their plight and need for assistance. Any help given is not charity, but simply a repayment of a debt we owe all indigenous people in our beloved country, for giving up their homes and way of life. Our strength as a nation is in our brotherhood to all citizens and love for our God. Most of all I dedicate all my creative abilities to my God. Without Him and His gift of love, I am lost. I am truly blessed by His love.

Tatanka Ska Son

Contents

ACKNOWLEDGEMENTS

This is a work of fiction. This book is the second in a series of novels about <u>The Chosen Ones Oglala Warriors,</u> involving three main characters of the Oglala Lakota Indian people. All of the characters, organizations, and events portrayed in this novel are either products of this author's imagination and/or used fictitiously.

I would like to thank most of all my wife for assistance in editing, her support of my work and for being my soul mate.

Many thanks go to Robert Seckman for his help in strengthening my knowledge of the Pine Ridge Reservation and some of the problems existing there. He has been a benefactor for the Oglala Lakota for years. He has also helped with editing.

A huge thank you goes to Doris Seckman for her unselfish effort in editing of this novel. I am most grateful for her support and encouragement.

I want thank both Robert and Doris for their boundless support and friendship, it means the world to me.

Others I thank for their editing and input are:

Tami A. Strosahl, my dear friend, I would like to thank her for technical support in creating the website and help with editing.

Thank you to my brother, Preston, for introducing me to Wanda Collins, whose hard work and perseverance made this book possible, by her years of experience in publishing, graphics and engraving. She also has a keen eye for editing.

Some BING artwork was used in this book.

Preface

The Chosen Ones Oglala Warriors

In the early 1980's this author became aware of some of the plights of the Oglala Lakota Indian people of the Pine Ridge Indian Reservation. Over the years since those earlier times, the plight of the Oglala Lakota Indians has moved my concerns for the welfare of the Oglala Lakota children to have hope and a faith in one who loves them.

Many of the children are abused, by the results of drug and alcohol overuse by parents, who suffer from lack of hope, primarily because of eighty-five percent unemployment among those on the reservation. This is a sad state of affairs and the citizens of this great country should direct more resources and attention to solving the problems of these fine people who lost their lands and culture to the pioneers who came long ago to take lands and resources for their own. They destroyed the hunting grounds, took the lands from the Indians, shut down their culture and ways of living in the arms of Mother Earth and following the customs of their forefathers, and used force to subjugate them to their religious beliefs. To believe in God is a choice of each individual, as stated in our Constitution. We did not give the American Indian these rights and they were stolen from them, and caused great damage to their culture, freedom to worship and live as they pleased, in the pursuit of happiness.

Their ancestral heritage was stolen, by the wašicun (white man). This is not a statement of fiction but a fact documented by our country's historical records. We, the American people, must honor our debt which we all owe to all indigenous American Indians.

Any help or assistance to better their living conditions, educational and career opportunities and social acceptance, is sorely needed at this time in our history, as a country, which was founded on "In God We Trust". This assistance should stand at the forefront of our charitable giving. We as good servants to humanity on a whole give billions of dollars in aid to foreign countries and that has been honorable. However, we should put our own people first, when they are taken care of, then any excess funds or other types of aid can go to those in need worldwide.

The purpose of this book series is to raise awareness of the American Indians and their needs, and to let them know there are those who may not be physical members of their tribe, but are tribal members in mind, spirit and heart. This author has chosen the Oglala Lakota people as his people to support.

This series is about the lives of three Oglala Lakota Indians as they grow up and their special relationship with Tatanka Ska Son (Jesus in the form of a white buffalo). This book series has many adventures and teaches some Lakota language and other dialects. The entire language and dialect meaning section for The Chosen Ones Oglala Warriors Dangerous Missions in the Northwest is listed in alphabetical order in the Appendix located in the back of the book.

The first book in the series of novels of The Chosen Ones Oglala Warriors is based on three main characters. They are young Oglala Lakota Indians, who meet a 'White Buffalo' that appears and makes them 'Story Tellers'. He follows them from boyhood to strong braves, advising and protecting them throughout their lives.

Book one, takes the three young Oglala Lakota Indians from boys to manhood as respected braves in their Oglala Lakota village. They earn the respect of the villagers and their chief by providing food for the villagers and their own tipis (teepee or tent or lodge). Most of all they are respected for their 'Story Telling', involving their many incredible experiences with Tatanka Ska Son, who has come to Mother Earth as a White Buffalo.

The Chosen Ones Oglala Warriors book series follows these three 'Chosen Ones' on adventures of hunting, fighting great grizzly bears, big wolves and other enemy Indian tribes, who come against them. They even rescue a Crow brave, who is being tortured, by Jicarilla Apache raiders.

This is book two in the series of The Chosen Ones Oglala Warriors entitled, Dangerous Missions in the Northwest, where we follow the three Oglala Lakota braves on new adventures. 'The Chosen Ones' take on a special mission to the far northwest of early America, with a new friend, the one they saved from the Jicarilla Apache some time ago, who has joined them. He has special powers from Wakantanka (God), which will prove very important to their mission's success.

The mission members will be mainly traveling up a great river heading west. They will meet many tribes in their travels, some friendly, some warlike. This entire series of novels, will educate about Mother Earth's wonders and its wildlife, along with teaching some Lakota dialect, and with some other tribal words. Those who read will learn some good manners from the Oglala Lakota Indians and their many customs, along with some character building traits and love for the Children of Wakantanka.

There are many stories yet to be told by <u>The Chosen Ones Oglala Warriors</u> in this book series, who have each been given special powers by Wakantanka to deal with the dangers that lie ahead in their many missions.

This book series is for anyone who loves adventure and the American Indian culture, along with learning about honor, respect and character-building traits through 'Campfire Story Telling'. Thank you for your support. Keep the campfires burning, and may Wakantanka Bless You.

Jerry Barrett

Chapter 1

Okiziwakiya Renamed

An early morning sunrise finds Okiziwakiya (cause to heal up – Lakota dialect), Luzahan (swift – Lakota dialect) and Ciqala (little one – Lakota dialect) returning from their battle against the Jicarilla Apache (Jicarilla Apache, one of several loosely organized autonomous bands of the Eastern Apache), —refers to members of the Jicarilla Apache Nation currently living in New Mexico and speaking a Southern Athabaskan language— and their new Chief Cougar (Ndolkan – Jicarilla Apache dialect) Man (Homme – Jicarilla Apache dialect). It was a great victory for the three young braves, along with their Crow friend Sun (Axxaashe – Crow dialect) Man (Bachhee – Crow dialect) including his braves and Okiziwakiya's animal brothers, Grizzly Bear (Mato Ḣota – Lakota dialect) Brother (Titakuye – immediate relatives – Lakota dialect) –Grizzly Bear Brother–, Šungmanitu (a wolf – Lakota dialect) Aitancan (the ruler over – Lakota dialect) –Wolf Ruler– and his pack of wolves.

Three young braves Okiziwakiya, Luzahan and Ciqala enter their village followed by their animal brothers of the deep woods and all the Oglala Lakota villagers start to cheer with chants of welcome. Okiziwakiya leads the small army straight to Chief Matoskah's (white bear – Lakota dialect) tipi (teepee or lodge or tent – Lakota dialect).

Chief Matoskah emerges from his tipi and greets his son with a warm hug. "You worry your mother my son, but not your father, as he knows you walk with Wakantanka by your side," says the Oglala Lakota chief. Chief Matoskah calls for all the villagers to welcome the returning warrior braves and their animal allies and have a campfire story telling by Okiziwakiya later that night. The entire village is buzzing with excitement to hear what adventure these special braves and their animal brothers have to share at the giant campfire, as darkness draws over their village.

The entire village has gathered around a huge campfire and are eating tatanka (a male buffalo – Lakota dialect) meat, boiled beans, and roasted corn. When most have finished eating, Chief Matoskah stands and all goes silent as he raises both hands high and begins to speak "I will speak, and do so with great joy in my heart. My son, Okiziwakiya, has told me of his great victory, which he will tell all who will listen after I have spoken. It is my wish to give my son a new name, which bears much honor, as I honor him. From this day forward Okiziwakiya will be known as Wanagiyata (in the land of spirits – Lakota dialect) and that is all I have to say."

All the villagers cheer and surround Wanagiyata and congratulate him and urge him to start his story telling. It is late before Wanagiyata finishes his story and then Luzahan and Ciqala tell their stories. No one has left and when Ciqala finishes his story telling, the entire village cheers and chant honoring the three young braves. Bear Brother and Wolf Ruler are fast asleep, having filled their bellies; one šungmanitu is awake and watches over the villagers with the outside camp guard by his side. It has been a great day in the Oglala Lakota village.

Wanagiyata wakes up from a good night's sleep to the smell of cooked tatanka soup with some greens his mother Winona (first born daughter – Lakota dialect) has cooked for him, her way of blessing him with her service and love as his mother. He wakes up from a dream he has been having about Wachiwi (dancing girl – Lakota dialect). She seems to be on his mind more each day and now in his dreams.

Wanagiyata is starting to weaken in his resolve of the value of freedom from responsibility and is considering asking for Wachiwi's hand in marriage, but also does not have gifts to give to her father, Cetan Tánka (the big hawk – Lakota dialect), in order for him to wipeya (sell – Lakota dialect) Wachiwi to him for marriage. Wanagiyata must think about this more, as he is very committed to his work of storytelling and adventure, besides he must increase his ownership of horses, as he only has two to offer now and he feels that is not enough to honor his offer for Wachiwi's hand in marriage.

Wanagiyata may ask Wachiwi's father what he would ask for her, maybe because of his standing in the tribe, her father might accept less than he might ask of another brave. Maybe, he will ask later, he would rather have more to offer for her hand in marriage. He thanks his mother for the tatanka soup and enjoys a warm early meal, thanks to his dear mother Winona and her loving service to him. He is thinking he should go fishing and bring Winona her favorite food hogleglega (the grass pike, or perhaps also, the rainbow fish – Lakota dialect) that would please her greatly.

Wanagiyata waits for his mother to leave their tipi and then gathers his fishing arrows, bow, spear and tomahawk and leaves for his favorite fishing area. Winter is just weeks away and he dresses in his taha (a deerskin – Lakota dialect) pants and tatanka robe, which he will sleep in if needed, along with some sintehanska (whitetail deer – Lakota dialect) jerky and mni (water – Lakota dialect) walega (the bladder – Lakota dialect) canteen. He has decided to go alone and do some deep thinking in silence, while he fishes.

Wanagiyata travels on foot and is very close to his chosen spot on the river some miles from his village; when he is suddenly surrounded by twelve Chippewa renegade braves and does not have a chance to defend against them. These Chippewa braves have been scouting Wanagiyata's village and were not part of Chief Bagwungijik's (hole in the sky – Chippewa dialect) war party that tried to attack the Oglala Lakota village months ago. They are now friends to the Oglala Lakota and would not have allowed this evil to come against their new friends.

Their leader is Abooksigun (wildcat – Chippewa dialect) a wild minded brave of big frame, whose name fits him well. He is planning to try to use his new prisoner to trade for horses, but first he will torture his prisoner. In order that his own warriors will fear him and his cruelty and power even more and be more willing to obey his every command, without hesitation.

Wanagiyata is bound by deerskin straps to a large tree and Abooksigun orders his braves to take turns shooting arrows as close to Wanagiyata as they can without hitting him. The first brave aims his arrow above Wanagiyata's head and just misses by about a foot, Wanagiyata does not flinch or show fear and the next brave takes aim at his right ear and comes within two inches, and still no reaction of fear is shown by the Wanagiyata. After all braves have taken turns shooting arrows at Wanagiyata, Abooksigun takes his turn and shoots his arrow at Wanagiyata's left thigh and hits him high in the left thigh and his arrow goes through Wanagiyata's thigh and embeds itself deep into the tree. Wanagiyata still does not show any emotion or sign of suffering. All the braves are silent and seem impressed by the prisoner's brave display of emotional control.

Abooksigun is not impressed and orders a fire to be made, believing that his fire test he plans to subject his prisoner to, will make Wanagiyata cry-out in pain. Before Abooksigun can apply a fire brand (burning torch – English language), petuspe (a firebrand – Lakota dialect) to

11

Wanagiyata, grizzly bear brother, Mato Hota Titakuye, charges in and attacks the raiding party swatting them with his big powerful paws sending them flying like small birds in a wind storm. Abooksigun shoots two arrows from his bow into Mato Hota Titakuye, before fleeing with two other Chippewa braves deep into the woods, leaving their silent brothers behind.

Mato Hota Titakuye goes to Wanagiyata and chews the deerskin straps binding him to the large tree freeing his Oglala Lakota brother. Wanagiyata breaks off the arrow, leaving the arrowhead embedded in the tree and pulls the remaining arrow shaft out of his leg showing no pain, as he did not feel any pain at any time. His wound closes and he is healed, for Wakantanka (God – Lakota dialect) watches over him, as they walk together in a shared spirit.

Wanagiyata thanks his bear brother for saving him and then pulls the two arrows from his belly and right shoulder very carefully and slowly. When he removes the arrows, he does so, without leaving the arrowheads in his dear brother Mato Hota Titakuye, who feels no pain as he is treated by Wanagiyata. Both brothers in nature realize Wakantanka has been with them and is with them now. They both bow down and give thanks to Wakantanka. They make camp for the night as sunset closes in. They will head back to Wanagiyata's village tomorrow.

Meanwhile, Abooksigun is hiding with his two Chippewa braves nearby. He is very angry and tells his braves he will go to the Oglala Lakota village and take some women prisoners as slaves. Both Chippewa braves do not want to help, but fear

Abooksigun and follow him to the Oglala Lakota village and scout the guards on duty near the village outskirts. They have watched for young maidens and spotted two that Abooksigun likes enter their tipis for the night.

The three Chippewa wait until night's darkness sets in and the villagers are quiet and asleep. Then they slip in on the guard and hit him in the head with rock, knocking him unconscious and then they creep up to the backside of the first tipi. Abooksigun and his Chippewa braves slip under the back of the family tipi of Wachiwi and swiftly kill her father and mother and knock Wachiwi out, bind and gag her. Then the three carry her very quietly out into the woods and go to the other young maiden's tipi they have scouted and kill the parents of Kimimila (butterfly – Lakota dialect) and she is silenced by the swift hard fist of Abooksigun.

The three Chippewa braves make their way with their two new prisoners deep into the forest, putting many miles between them and the Oglala Lakota village, before their evil deeds have been discovered by other Oglala Lakota villagers. Their evil deeds will cause great sorrow in the Oglala Lakota village when the night guard recovers and warns the villagers.

Mato Hota Titakuye is loping along at a good pace heading back to the Oglala Lakota village, with Wanagiyata riding on his broad back, hanging on to his long fur. Wanagiyata is thinking about warning his father about the evil Chippewa raiders, who are planning trouble and have tortured him. He will seek his father's council and decide, if he needs to follow the remaining Chippewa braves and capture or kill them, with his father's blessing.

Mato Hota Brother reaches the Oglala Lakota village and

enters heading toward Chief Matoskah's tipi. He is standing holding the bridle of his šungbloka (stallion - male horse – Lakota dialect). All the village is alive, as many braves gather their weapons and šunkawakans (a horse – Lakota dialect) making ready to go and rescue the two young maidens taken as prisoners and avenge the killing of their parents.

Wanagiyata has arrived just in time to be involved in this rescue mission. When he finds out about what has happened, he suffers from the knowledge that the three Chippewa, who made the raid on the Oglala Lakota village, were the ones he believed were, in fact, those he thought were fleeing away from him and his grizzly brother, Mato Hota Titakuye, leaving his fellow braves behind in such a show of cowardice. He feels he should have gone after them and this terrible killing and taking of prisoners would not have happened. The weight of his self-blame weighs heavy on his heart and he is filled with resolve and urgency to recover Wachiwi and Kimimila.

A Oglala Lakota rescue party of twenty braves are formed and arm themselves and are ready to follow Chief Matoskah. Wanagiyata pulls his father aside and asks him to stay in the village, in case there may be more Chippewa coming against the village and they may need his leadership. Then further, he asked of his father, if he may lead the rescue party in his place. Chief Matoskah replies, "My son, I have heard your council. Your words have wisdom beyond your ojilaka (the offspring, the young ones of both men and animals – Lakota dialect) and iwatohantu (sometime, one day in reference to something – Lakota dialect) you will lead our Oglala Lakota people. Take my place and bring our Oglala Lakota maidens back to their people." Chief Matoskah announces, that he will stay and guard the village and that Wanagiyata will lead the rescue party. A loud shout goes up in approval of the words of their chief and this gives Wanagiyata a feeling of confidence.

Wanagiyata and his braves have been tracking the Chippewa on horseback with scouts out front to guide them, switching off in order to keep up a strong pace moving forward. They are aided by their brother, Šungmanitu Aitancan, and six of his wolf pack who have joined in tracking of the Chippewa, running out on each side of the scouts and trackers, keeping them directly on the trail of the captors and their prisoners.

Meanwhile, Abooksigun is thinking of slowing down, he has put many miles between them and the Oglala Lakota village. He decides to make a cold camp at sunset. His two Chippewa braves are very glad to stop and rest, as they have been pushed to make good time forcing their young Oglala Lakota maidens forward. They have had to carry them many times and have also, beaten them in order to make them move and keep pace with their leader, Abooksigun. He has no patience with any slacking by anyone to his orders.

After the three Chippewa have eaten some dried jerky and rested awhile and having kept watch on their prisoners, Abooksigun orders his two braves to stand guard, two hours on and two hours off. He will rest all night and regain his strength. Wachiwi and Kimimila have not been offered any food, only water, to keep them going for two days. They are very scared and are hoping and praying to Wakantanka to help them and keep them safe from torture or any harm.

Šungmanitu Ruler begins howling to his scouting pack members and they answer him back yelping from each side of  the Oglala Lakota trackers. He breaks off from running beside Wanagiyata and races ahead of the scouts and disappears from sight. Wolf Ruler has the Chippewa scent deep in his nostrils and is closing in on them at a rapid pace. He knows he is getting close and slows down to a walk and finally he hears one of the Oglala Lakota maiden's moan in pain from her bound wrists, he stops and begins to crawl toward the sound he has heard in the dark night. He turns and quietly retraces his tracks for about two hundred yards distance and make his trail with his scent, by rolling over many times in a circle and sprays his scent on the spot. Wolf Ruler runs back toward his Oglala Lakota brothers and his wolf pack warriors.

Šungmanitu Ruler runs up to Wanagiyata, and by sign language lets him know, he has found the Chippewa and that they are close by. The rescue party has picked up the pace following Šungmanitu Ruler as he leads them forward toward the Chippewa campsite. The rescue party slows down as their wolf brother slows down and begins to walk slowly and then he stops and returns to let Wanagiyata know they are close to the enemy.

Wanagiyata orders five braves to hold the horses back and keep them quiet and he leads his fifteen remaining Oglala Lakota braves forward, as he follows his šungmanitu brother toward the Chippewa campsite. When Šungmanitu Ruler comes to his scent marking, he lets Wanagiyata know they are very close and Wanagiyata whispers to his braves to spread out and try to encircle the Chippewa cold camp and move up closer and wait for his signal to close in on the Chippewa raiders.

It is about one hour before sunrise and Abooksigun, is awakened by the moaning of Wachiwi and feeling rested, he is thinking of the beauty of his moaning prisoner and decides to try and force her to love him, as he plans to make her his slave. He gets up and goes over to Wachiwi and unties her and starts to try and kiss her, she screams and fights him, but he is stronger than her and he slaps her and then tries to kiss her again, again she fights him.

Wanagiyata gives the signal to attack and rushes in jumping on Abooksigun with his hunting knife, smashing him to the ground with his knife blade at his throat. Wolf Ruler has torn out the throat of one of the Chippewa braves and the other remaining Chippewa brave has been taken prisoner by other Oglala Lakota braves, as he tried to escape.

Wanagiyata has his braves bind Abooksigun and the surviving Chippewa brave together back to back. Wachiwi goes to Kimimila and unties her and they both hug each other and comfort one another in a joyous celebration of being saved by their tribal members. Both Oglala Lakota maidens hold each other as a campfire is made and they can see more clearly. Both young maidens now approach Wanagiyata and Kimimila is first to hug him, and express her heart felt gratitude, for being saved, from the Chippewa raiders. Next, Wachiwi closes in facing him, she kneels and reaches up taking both his hands and kisses each one. Wanagiyata pulls her to her feet and hugs her showing much affection and respect for her, for she has been lost to him for too long and he feared for her safety.

Now he is very thankful that she is safe in his arms and he

feels a warm feeling he has never known before and he does not want this feeling to go away. He holds her close and rocks back and forth, side to side with her, as he hugs her tightly.

It is a time of joy and a time to thank Wakantanka, which Wanagiyata calls for silence and offers up a prayer, as he is holding Wachiwi and Kimimila, thanking Wakantanka for this great moment in time, where great joy is shared by rescuers and victims alike. It is a very special time.

Wanagiyata calls for camp to be made by a nearby river and his rescue party is glad to have rest and care for their horses, who have been running long and hard in the chase to catch up to the Chippewa raiders. Now he personally tends the injuries of Wachiwi and Kimimila by their bonds of deerskin bindings and scratches from being pulled though bushes and dragged on the ground. He has carried some healing leaves and ointment his mother Winona has made up for him, to be carried by him for any healing duties he may need to administer to any wounded or injured he may come upon. Wanagiyata is still known among his oyate (a people, nation, or tribe – Lakota dialect) tribe as a great healer, which he has proven himself to be many times, with the help of Tatanka Ska Son (Son of Wakantanka), and His Father, Wakantanka.

While Wanagiyata is treating a wound on young Kimimila's long slender right leg just above the knee, Ciqala is hovering over her along with Luzahan. Kimimila is looking at Wanagiyata, as he cleans and treats her deep scratch with his healing ointment. She looks up at Ciqala more than once and gives him a bright smile. Kimimila is a tall slender pretty young maiden of fourteen, a good friend of Wachiwi and, she has had her eye on Ciqala for at least a year. She is taller than he is, but she sees a strength in him and feels he is brave and carries a good heart, or Wanagiyata would not consider him a close brother. He must be a good brave and she will show him favor whenever she can, not being too bold in doing so, as Oglala Lakota customs require.

Ciqala is smitten, but needs time to live without anything or personal feelings to get in his way as he follows his brothers Wanagiyata and Luzahan in the adventures they share as new Oglala Lakota braves, earning the respect of their villagers and the Elders. However, romance is blooming, just as the wildflowers spring up through a late snow in early springtime, they find a way to blossom. Time tells all stories true. This 'Campfire Story Telling' is yet to come.

The rescuers camp settles down for the night listening to the soothing sounds of rushing water as it glides over rocks and around great borders in its journey to the ocean many moons ride by horseback from where they camp. Wanagiyata has asked Wolf Ruler to sleep close to Wachiwi and Kimimila and keep them safe and warm. He looks over to see them all huddled together and sleeping near a campfire, which he will keep supplied with wood during the night, to insure their comfort. He will sleep very little as he is thinking about what to do about the loss of the parents of his new charges, the orphaned Oglala Lakota maidens and his two murdering Chippewa braves, who must be dealt justice for their evil deeds.

Wanagiyata leaves the warmth of his blanket twice during the night to fuel the campfire with wood, all under the watchful eye of Šungmanitu Ruler who sleeps with one eye open most of the time. He also, checks the guards he has posted around the perimeter of his camp, as he does often not taking any chances, that any other Chippewa may be in the area. Šungmanitu Ruler has posted some of his pack further out from the camp, to watch for any enemy, who might come upon the Oglala Lakota campsite.

All is well as Wanagiyata climbs under his blanket in the early morning hours and he prays to Wakantanka for guidance in his decisions. When he wakes from a dream to the sound of a popping in his campfire, which interrupts his deep sleeps. He has the answers he has been praying for, drawn from his dream, and he is renewed with energy and resolve. He wakes the camp and instructs everyone to eat, break camp and head back to the Oglala Lakota village and their warm tipis.

Wanagiyata pulls Wachiwi up behind him on his šunkawakan and instructs Ciqala to give Kimimila a ride behind him, which brings a big smile from Kimimila and slight sheepish smile from Ciqala, not to give away his feelings totally to other braves watching him and her closely. Wanagiyata is aware of Kimimila's feelings and wants her to have some joy, as the loss of her family and the hardship she has suffered at the hands of the Chippewa has overwhelmed her with sorrow. He knows she will be pleased to ride behind the respected young warrior Ciqala.

The Oglala Lakota rescue party head back toward their village with the two Chippewa raiders bound and made to walk at a fast pace to keep up or they will be dragged on the ground until they can regain their footing. They both fall a number of times before reaching the Oglala Lakota village, and they experience a little of the pain and suffering they put the Oglala Lakota maidens through.

The sound of great celebration goes up from the Oglala

Lakota villagers, as the rescue party moves through the village toward Chief Matoskah's tipi. Wanagiyata is leading the two Chippewa raiders behind his horse and when Chief Matoskah emerges from his tipi, he raises his hands high and all goes totally quiet as he begins to speak. "Welcome my son, Wanagiyata, and all Oglala Lakota braves, and animal brothers. Let there be a great gathering around a hinsko (so big, so large – Lakota dialect) campfire and many who will it so, will do the Wiwanyank Wacipi (Sundance – Lakota dialect). This is a great day and that is all I have to say," all directed to the villagers by the strong voice of Chief Matoskah. He motions for his son to come into his tipi and speak of his mission.

Wanagiyata speaks to his father of all the rescue details and then tells his father that he has prayed to Wakantanka for wisdom concerning what action he should take to insure the future care for Wachiwi and Kimimila. He tells his father, Chief Matoskah, his thoughts, which suggest that he wishes his father and mother, would consider bringing Wachiwi into their tipi as a daughter. Wanagiyata would leave there tipi and live in Wachiwi's parent's tipi. All, so no rumors or suspicions would be cast upon the reputation of Wachiwi. He will suggest that Chief Matoskah speak with Ciqala's parents and ask them to take Kimimila in as their daughter and let Ciqala move in to her parent's tipi. This action would help with the great loss both girls are going through and they would have the care and love of a new family. Chief Matoskah agrees with this his son's reasoning, as he knows his son walks with Wakantanka and His Son, Tatanka Ska Son.

The next thought within Wanagiyata's judgment, he shares with his father is what he feels may be the best way they should deliver justice fairly with their murdering evil Chippewa prisoners. He shares with his father, the fact that many Oglala Lakota tribe members will want to punish and kill them, as would be the normal way of handling them under Oglala Lakota customs and ways. However, after praying to Wakantanka, Wanagiyata feels that if Chief Matoskah were to take a small peace party of Oglala Lakota braves and return the two evil murders to Chippewa Chief Bagwungijik. He would be welcomed now that they are at peace with the Chippewa. Let the Chippewa deal with them as is their custom for justice among their people.

This act of honoring the Chippewa oyate would please them and further enhance the feeling of trust between former enemies, who are now at peace. Wanagiyata also feels, it will help show

the Oglala Lakota people are both a merciful and fair-minded people, who do not favor revenge justice over true justice, as Wakantanka would consider just and honorably carried out. "These are my words and my judgment my father, after my prayer visit with Wakantanka. What do you council mighty chief and it shall be done"? asked Wanagiyata.

Chief Matoskah considers all words of his son and thinks of the wisdom within those words and is silent for some time thinking deeply, before he answers his son's request. Chief Matoskah speaks, "Your words are not the words of a koškala (a young man – Lakota dialect) of few seasons of being a brave, you also speak as a wahununpa (man in the sacred language – Lakota dialect) and your wisdom honors me as your father. Truly, your new name and actions seem wakipuskil iyeya (to make join suddenly together – Lakota dialect). I will do as you have counseled me, my son."

Dancing Girl (Wachiwi) and Butterfly (Kimimila) both are joyous with Chief Matoskah's offer and that of Ciqala's parents and move in to live with them. Now both Wanagiyata and Ciqala are living alone in their new tipis. They are becoming true independent braves, well on their own and must pick up some of the duties, their dear mothers have taught them.

Luzahan has the best of both worlds now, he has his mother's attention and care, and he can visit his brothers and stay with them any time he feels a need for their fellowship and the telling of stories and with the embellishment as needed, which bring much laughter and aikpablaya (to make a fool of one's self by talking or acting foolishly – Lakota dialect) talking. Their friendship is a blessing, which is a gift we all should strive to achieve in our own short life's journey upon our dear Mother Earth, for it is truly the love for others and not love of self, which is the strength and solid foundation of friendship and great joy.

May Wakantanka Bless You greatly. Remember His love and thank Him in your prayers and you will find favor. Until our next Campfire Story Telling – "Chief Matoskah's Journey to the Chippewa Village of Chief Bagwungijik," stay strong and safe.

MOTHER EARTH'S SONG

I come to you at my Father's Wakantanka's (God - Lakota) hand
My winds I send to you from mountains high
To fill your lungs with life's breath
That you may live in my care
Where nature's gifts you share with many

The wi (sun – Lakota) which brings all seasons
Smiles its warmth in all directions you may follow
In the four corners I set before you
That your path may be clear
In the journey of life

Look for the dakota (allies or friend) I surround you with
Treat them yuonihan (to honor, treat with attention)
That you may be takolaku (his special friend)
This I sing to you in all tongues to be heard by all oyate (a people,
nation, tribe, or band)

I bring for you pure mni (water) waters cold
To run away your dry thirst and give you life
Where none would be
Listen to her song as she sings over the rocks
In a fast water mountain stream

Walk softly in your taha (deerskin) hanpa (moccasins)
Let no wicaša (man, a man, mankind) wawašagya (render worthless)
These gifts of song I give to you so freely
Let no evil ahinhan (to rain upon, to fall as rain does on things) upon
your spirit
That I may not feel acantešilyakel (sadly or sorrowfully for) you
This is my Lakota song I sing as Mother Earth, hear me

Jerry Barrett

Chapter 2

Chief Matoskah's Journey to the <u>*Chippewa Village of Chief Bagwungijik*</u>

Snow is soon to visit the small Oglala Lakota village —now located in present day South Dakota—. The signs of winter are in the air as it blows cool, touching golden leaves and twisting them loose to dance their final death dance drifting to the ground, where they will enrich the forest floor and cover and protect seeds planted by Mother Earth from the blanket of heavy snows to come for the long winter season.

Chief Matoskah (white bear) is making ready with twelve

Oglala Lakota braves to return two renegade Chippewa prisoners back to Chief Bagwungijik (hole in the sky – Chippewa dialect) for them to use their tribal laws to punish the two killers his son Wanagiyata (in the land of spirits) has captured while rescuing two young Oglala Lakota maidens, who were taken prisoner by renegade raiders, led by Abooksigun (wildcat – Chippewa dialect). He was leading a small band of Chippewa raiders that, were on their way to steal horses, from the Oglala Lakota village, and ran into Wanagiyata, who was on a fishing trip.

They captured him and were about to burn him with a petuspe (a fire brand), when Wanagiyata's grizzly bear brother, Mato Hota (grizzly bear) Titakuye (immediate relatives), rushed in and killed all but Abooksigun and two other Chippewa braves who escaped. Abooksigun and his two not so willing braves, snuck back to Wanagiyata's village before he returned and killed the parents of Wachiwi (dancing girl) and Kimimila (butterfly) and took them prisoner before fleeing away.

When Wanagiyata returned and found out what had happened, he was able to persuade his father, Chief Matoskah, to let him lead a rescue party and bring back the two Oglala Lakota maidens. Wanagiyata's rescue party had the help of his wolf brother Šungmanitu (a wolf) Aitancan (ruler) and some of his wolf pack, who tracked down Abooksigun and his two Chippewa braves. As they rushed in, Šungmanitu Aitancan was first to attack and killed one of the Chippewa braves. Wanagiyata rushed Abooksigun, winning in hand to hand combat and took him prisoner, along with the other remaining Chippewa brave and returned them to the Oglala Lakota village, for Chief Matoskah to deal out justice.

Chief Matoskah was ready to have the evil Chippewa braves

face death for their evil deeds, but Wanagiyata had a dream and was advised by Wakantanka to take the two prisoners back to their own Chippewa village and give them over to Chief Bagwungijik, whom the Oglala Lakota were now at peace with. Wanagiyata shared his experience; he had, in a dream, with Wakantanka (God). He shares this dream with his father and Chief Matoskah agrees that this would show good will toward the Chippewa people. Then they could deal justice to the renegade outcast of their oyate (a people, nation, or tribe) according to their custom.

Chief Matoskah leaves with his son, Wanagiyata, and puts the medicine man, Takoda (friend to everyone – Lakota dialect), in charge of the village. The chief takes twelve extra braves with him, two of which are Luzahan (swift - to be fast, fast running) and Ciqala (little one), who are in charge of the Chippewa prisoners, a duty they gladly accept. The peace party leaves the village as the villagers stand in silence; watch them pass through their village. All remain silent and no one yells at the killers or taunts them, even though they have taken the lives of four Oglala

 Lakota they loved. This is the respect they have for Chief Matoskah and what he would wish to be so, not to mention Wanagiyata, who displays honor and respect in all his actions. Tatanka Ska Son (Son of Wakantanka) has taught him well and he must pass that forward in his example before his oyate.

It is hard for both Luzahan and Ciqala to treat the prisoners they are charged to guard and care for with any kindness, but they know that Tatanka Ska Son would be sure to treat them with

kindness and care for them as they travel toward the Chippewa village. Abooksigun cannot believe he has not been tortured and killed and does not understand this itokeca (to be altered – Lakota dialect) of the Oglala Lakota customs concerning the application of punishment of crimes.

Abooksigun realizes, that he will be dealt with by his people and that is of no comfort to him as he has been an outcast from his Chippewa people for two winters time, along with twelve braves who went with him to become renegades, raiding all villages and hunting parties they could overcome. He is feeling some regret at his life choice and his only fellow tribal brave is very mad at him for forcing him to be part of his great crime of killing and kidnapping. He may try his luck at escaping, if given the chance.

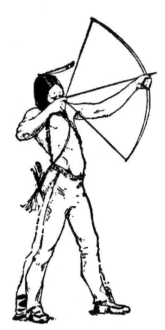

The peace party has been traveling for two days on horseback, with their prisoners walking. Luzahan is leading Abooksigun and Ciqala has charge of the other Chippewa prisoner. Chief Matoskah calls a halt and the prisoners are given food and drink along with the Oglala Lakota braves. Abooksigun speaks asking Wanagiyata to untie him, so he can ocesli (to defecate in – Lakota dialect) the woods by himself and Wanagiyata understands him and unties him, as he has before for this purpose. Wanagiyata watches as Abooksigun goes behind a bush for some privacy. Abooksigun does not relieve himself, but instead takes off running as fast as he can. He makes about five horse lengths before he is brought down by an arrow high in his left leg.

Wanagiyata has been expecting a trick from Abooksigun and had his arrow at the ready in his bow. Abooksigun is pulled up from the ground and returned to Chief Matoskah, where he faces the chief. "You are not going to be free of punishment by your people, Abooksigun. What would you have us do with this dishonorable wicaša (man – Lakota dialect) Wanagiyata"? asks Chief Matoskah. Wanagiyata walks up to Abooksigun and reaches for the arrow he shot deep in Abooksigun's leg and pulls it out, with arrowhead and shaft intact.

Abooksigun never felt any pain and is totally amazed at what he has just experienced and seen with his own eyes. He looks into Wanagiyata's eyes and sees mercy and kindness and he is overcome by the wonder of this man and feels he is looking into the eyes of a sacred one, with no doubt in his mind.

Abooksigun kneels and crosses his arms in a submissive manner to show respect and honor to him that has healed him and probably saved his life. Wanagiyata pulls Abooksigun to his feet and tells him in his own tongue —dialect— of Chippewa, that he must not try that again or he will be punished. Abooksigun agrees by shaking his head in sign language.

Chief Matoskah has been worrying about his decision to leave the medicine man, Takoda, in charge, while he is gone. He feels the medicine man may not be as wise in defending the village if it comes under attack. Chief Matoskah tells his son to take two other braves and return to the village immediately and take over as leader of the Oglala Lakota village, until he returns from the Chippewa village. Wanagiyata turns and leaves with two braves and heads back at all speed to the Oglala Lakota village.

Three days later the peace party has reached the outskirts of the Chippewa village of Chief Bagwungijik and are escorted by many Chippewa braves through their village, as many villagers watch in wonderment at the sight of the Oglala Lakota and their Chippewa prisoners. Chief Bagwungijik comes out to greet Chief Matoskah, as if he is a long lost Chippewa brother, and this action by their chief causes all the villagers to relax wiping away any apprehensions they were experiencing with the strangers of the Oglala Lakota Nation among them. Chief Bagwungijik invites Chief Matoskah, Luzahan and Ciqala into his tipi (teepee or tent or lodge) to smoke the peace pipe and have council to discuss the reason for bringing in the two outcast Chippewa braves.

Chief Bagwungijik listens to Chief Matoskah's story and expresses his sorrow for the loss of lives among the Oglala Lakota and assures Chief Matoskah that they will be dealt with, as the Elders decide fitting punishment for the crimes committed, which would most certainly mean torture and a hard death of suffering.

Chief Bagwungijik has a young daughter, who has fallen off a cliff and broken her back. She is paralyzed and is suffering with constant pain, as she lays motionless in the family tipi with her mother by her side. Once in a while, she makes a moaning sound and is sorry and makes a soft apology to her father for interrupting him and his guest with her noise of suffering. Chief Matoskah hears this moaning and asks about her plight. Chief Bagwungijik tells him the story of her accident and that he feels she is doomed to suffer until she dies and during this story telling, a tear creeps from his left eye and down his cheek.

Chief Matoskah is deeply touched by this story and tells him he will return to his Oglala Lakota village and send his son, Wanagiyata, back to see if he can help the daughter of Chief Bagwungijik, the young Gidagaakoons (fawn – Chippewa dialect). She is very beautiful and young Luzahan upon hearing this story has moved to her side and taken her hand in his and bowed his head in a prayer to Wakantanka, to heal her broken back.

Her father is touched by this kind act and offers for him to stay until Wanagiyata comes back to their village. Luzahan, ask Chief Matoskah if he can stay to pray for her and learn more of the Chippewa customs and see the Elders judgment of Abooksigun crimes.

Chief Matoskah gives Luzahan his blessing and asks to forgo any celebration of his visit. He merely wants to eat then return to send his son, Wanagiyata, so he can try to help his daughter Gidagaakoons without further delay.

This gesture of concern for Gidagaakoons by Chief Matoskah deeply touches the heart of Chief Bagwungijik. He orders in food and cold water for his honored guest and then Chief Matoskah and Ciqala along with his remaining braves leave for their village in great haste upon their fast horses.

Chief Bagwungijik has his son, Ma'iingan (timber wolf – Chippewa dialect), come and take charge over the welfare of Luzahan and let him share his tipi and show all manner of hospitality to this young Oglala Lakota brave until Wanagiyata comes to their Chippewa village. Luzahan goes to the side of Gidagaakoons every day in early morning and just before sunset and prays over her. Her smiles and radiance, even though in severe pain, is a testament to her character and mental strength and Luzahan finds himself drawn to her. This has happened by some unknown power he has not felt before. He wishes he could speak her Chippewa dialect, like his brother Wanagiyata can, but he does use sign language as much as he can to communicate with her. He will be glad when his brother returns and asks Wakantanka to heal her and then he can also interpret for him. He has some things to say to her that are weighing on his mind constantly, as he gets to know her without the help of the spoken word.

Two weeks have passed and the Chippewa Elders have met and pronounced a sentence of death by torture for Abooksigun. This judgment of guilt comes rapidly once voted on by the members of the Elders and the sentence is to be carried out the next day at midafternoon, before the entire Chippewa villagers, who are required to witness justice, as a lesson to all that doing evil does not bring a good result.

The day of punishment has come two weeks after the Elders have called for the death of Abooksigun and his fellow brave. Both braves are tied to poles placed in the ground with their hands tied behind them. The villagers are quiet, but a few women have been given the task of torturing these condemned Chippewa braves, by running around and poking them with sharp sticks. The village women have just started to torture the captive braves, when Wanagiyata comes riding into the Chippewa village on his šunkawakan (a horse). He has ridden hard and fast to get to the Chippewa village, along with two other Oglala Lakota braves.

All the torturing of the murders is halted by Chief Bagwungijik. The chief welcomes Wanagiyata and orders the two prisoners to be untied and held in a tipi until he orders their punishment to resume. Wanagiyata is glad to see the torture stopped, because he knows Wakantanka does not like torture

32

when it is unnecessary in the taking of life as that is the ultimate in punishment in and of itself.

Chief Bagwungijik brings his guest into his tipi and introduces him to his daughter joined by Luzahan, who is overjoyed to see his brother Oglala Lakota. The two brothers hug

and then Chief Bagwungijik introduces Wanagiyata to his daughter Gidagaakoons. Wanagiyata takes Gidagaakoons's left hand in his right hand and speaks to her in her Chippewa dialect, "Gidagaakoons, I am going to call on my God, Wakantanka. The only God to heal you and you may pray to Him silently as I do out loud." Luzahan takes her other hand as Wanagiyata lifts his head and looks upward and prays for the healing power of Wakantanka to flow though him.

After a few moments, Wanagiyata feels a warm feeling flow though his whole body and out to the young and beautiful Gidagaakoons. She feels all pain drain away and feeling returns swiftly to her legs. Wanagiyata asks Gidagaakoons to stand and walk to her mother, who is kneeling nearby. She stands with astonishment showing on her beautiful face and walks to her mother's side and lifts her to her feet. A great shouting takes over the entire tipi from all inside, with the exception of Wanagiyata, who remains kneeling and he offers thanks to Wakantanka and Tatanka Ska Son for this miracle of healing.

Chief Bagwungijik rushes from his tipi and shouts to all the villagers who are standing around waiting to see what would happen after the arrival of Wanagiyata, and he calls for a great celebration, as his daughter has been healed. It is a great day for Gidagaakoons and her family and all the Chippewa villagers.

All the villagers eat, dance, and sing all night long, with Gidagaakoons dancing among them. She finds Luzahan sitting by the large campfire beside Wanagiyata and his two Oglala Lakota braves who accompanied him. She indicates by sign language for him to dance along with the Chippewa villagers. He is hesitant, but cannot refuse her anything that could interfere with her joyous moment.

He is a quick learner and gets by with a credible Chippewa dance routine, with some of his own Oglala Lakota dance steps intertwined, keeping up with the beat of the Chippewa drums. All the while, Gidagaakoons watches closely dancing nearby his side. Wanagiyata and his fellow Oglala Lakota brave companions do have a little laughter sneak out once in a while, as Luzahan performs his dancing moves, some are no doubt newly invented by him to impress Gidagaakoons. There is great joy among all the villagers and their Oglala Lakota guests.

The next day in the late afternoon, Chief Bagwungijik again

orders each prisoner to be tied to a pole and for the women assigned to torture them, to begin by poking them with sharp sticks. Just as they begin, a great wind blows in and out of a bright blue tunnel of light that strikes the ground in front of Chief Bagwungijik comes the great figure of Tatanka Ska Son in all His glory. All the villagers are spellbound and all goes quiet. Tatanka Ska Son speaks in a strong deep Voice, "Bagwungijik, My Father, Wakantanka, has healed your daughter and wishes you to grant the life of these two, who have taken the life of your neighbors the Oglala Lakota people. It is His Wish that you let them face the judgment of one of My 'Chosen Ones', Wanagiyata, and let him judge their punishment." Chief Bagwungijik answers in a humble manner, "Tatanka Ska Son, I have felt Your mercy and forgiveness and surely it will be so, just as You say."

Wanagiyata is taken by surprise with this new assignment of great importance in so many ways. He must obey Tatanka Ska Son and His Father, Wakantanka, and Wanagiyata must appease the Chippewa people and their customs for these crimes committed along with the Oglala Lakota villagers, who have lost many friends by the evil hands of the prisoners guilty of murder and the kidnaping of Oglala Lakota maidens. He also, feels they should face a severe punishment for their crimes in his mind.

All the villagers are very quiet and everyone is looking at Wanagiyata including Tatanka Ska Son. Wanagiyata closes his eyes and lifts both hands high upward toward the red sky and silently asks Wakantanka for wisdom in this moment, as a great weight has been placed on him, with the lives of two Chippewa wicaša (to have reference to man) in his hands.

A long silence passes, as he prays for some time and then he kneels and bows his head for two minutes additional time. He slowly raises his head and stands tall and faces Tatanka Ska Son. Wanagiyata speaks, "Tatanka Ska Son, Your Father has told me to do, as You would do, and He told me to bring them before You and see if they will believe in You and ask for their lives, in order to serve You by traveling to all tribes in this great land and tell of Your greatness. They are to be 'Story Tellers' in Your Name for the rest of their lives. If when they look upon You and do not believe, they will surely die. That is my judgment and my wish, as Wakantanka has told me that would be your judgment, so let it be so." Chief Bagwungijik echoes with, "Let it be so, untie and bring the prisoners to face Tatanka Ska Son."

Abooksigun and his companion brave are placed on their knees before Tatanka Ska Son and He stares at each one with His big blue eyes and looks at their hearts. "Stand up now! Will you serve Me for the rest of your life by spreading the Words of My Father to all Indian nations, and do you repent of your murderous and evil ways? I see your heart, so answer truthfully," Tatanka Ska Son asks the prisoners. He looks into the eyes of Abooksigun and then the eyes of the other Chippewa prisoner.

Abooksigun's bindings fall off as he looks into Tatanka Ska Son's blue eyes and he falls to his knees in submission to the Will of Wakantanka's Son. The other brave looks at Tatanka Ska Son and appears to submit to His Will, but his heart is unrepentant. He falls forward face down dead, as a stone in winter's cold waters deep in the mountain river, before he hits the ground with a loud thud. A sound of amazement comes from

the mouths of all who watched this judgment and justice rendered by Tatanka Ska Son and the one who walks in the land of spirits, Wanagiyata.

All the Chippewa villagers, who have not seen Tatanka Ska Son before and the healing power of His chosen one, Wanagiyata, are truly in awe and all kneel, as Tatanka Ska Son flies up into the sky and slowly drifts away into an early sunset colored sky. All have now seen the Son of

Wakantanka and many will be believers before night finally takes them in deep sleep, much later in this night.

As night closes in on the Chippewa village, a great fire is built and all the villagers gather around, as Wanagiyata begins to tell the story of Tatanka Ska Son and Wakantanka and how Mother Earth was created and some stories of his adventures and rescues by Tatanka Ska Son. The entire village believes in Wakantanka and His Son,  Tatanka Ska Son, before Wanagiyata, Luzahan and his Oglala Lakota braves leave to return to their own village. But before they leave, there are words to be shared between Luzahan and Gidagaakoons and Wanagiyata has been commissioned with the task of interpreting for them.

Wanagiyata asks for permission from Chief Bagwungijik for Luzahan to speak to his daughter in a farewell meeting. He states that Chief Bagwungijik may attend to witness these meaningful words of farewell between these two young Indians members of different tribes and customs. The Chippewa chief gives his permission, and wishes to hear the words spoken between the two, to know their hearts and intentions toward one another.

The private talk is to be held in Chief Bagwungijik's tipi and his wife is also to be present. Luzahan knows he must choose his words wisely and hopefully still be able to express his feeling toward Gidagaakoons in a way that she will appreciate and that her parents will respect. The farewell talking will take place in the morning before the Oglala Lakota party leaves for their village.

Chief Bagwungijik's family, which now includes her brother Luzahan's friend Ma'iingan, has gathered with Wanagiyata, and Luzahan. Now Luzahan stands facing in a very serious manner, Gidagaakoons and says, "Gidagaakoons, your beauty and brightness of character have shown like the stars even as you suffered in great pain, your bright face would not show it in my presence. Your heart travels strong against the wind in an honest way. Your beauty would bring great sadness to never be seen again, for you have touched my heart as one of great value. When I leave your village, I will leave a part of me I cannot take from here. In another time, I will travel here in a journey of hope to find it is still a living thing and warm as it now lives in my mind."

Gidagaakoons listens closely as Wanagiyata interprets the words spoken by Luzahan, and she blushes as their eyes are fixed on one another. The meaning of Luzahan's words strikes deep within her heart. She looks at her father and mother and then to her brother for signs of responses to what Luzahan has said, then she speaks freely as she looks into his eyes, "You, swift one, Luzahan, with words I could not dream would come to my ears, will always be my friend. Upon your return to our Chippewa village, you will find the part you left with me; will be alive and warmer than when you left it near my blanket as you prayed for me. I give you a part of me to take on your path in life's journey on Mother Earth. Hold it well and listen to it sing to you, for it is yours to have." She hands him a small white feather from a male Bobwhite quail. Wanagiyata conveys the words to Luzahan and notices the faces of her family as he speaks. Wanagiyata sees an acceptance of all that has been spoken in this farewell between two young human beings of different tribes and customs.

Seeds have been planted in fertile soil, for a deep friendship thrives between the Oglala Lakota and the Chippewa people. Luzahan will think of her each time he hears the Bobwhite Quail sing from this day forward. How thoughtful was this small gift from Gidagaakoons and Luzahan will carry this small white quail feather always, very near to his heart tied on a deerskin string necklace he has fashioned for this purpose.

Meanwhile Abooksigun has been given jerky and mni (water) and sent away by Wanagiyata, to become a great 'Story Teller' for Wakantanka and His Son, Tatanka Ska Son, all through the mercy of Wanagiyata of the Spirit Land and the forgiveness of Tatanka Ska Son and His Father, Wakantanka.

May Wakantanka Bless You as you grow in His love and grace. Until our next Campfire Story Telling – "Wanagiyata's Great Mission of War."

Chapter 3

Wanagiyata's Great Mission of War

Late night in the Oglala Lakota village of Chief Matoskah (white bear), his son Wanagiyata (in the land of spirits) has just returned from his mission of healing the daughter of Chief Bagwungijik (hole in the sky – Chippewa dialect) chief of one of the tribes of the Chippewa Nation he has befriended. Wanagiyata is tired from his trip back home among his Oglala Lakota people and greets his mother and father briefly and then crawls into his blanket by a warm low burning fire. He spends the night in his parent's tipi (teepee or lodge or tent), because his tipi is cold from lack of use, while he was away on his mission of mercy.

He awakes to the smell of tatanka (a male buffalo – Lakota dialect) and vegetables in his favorite food; his mother cooks for his early meal. It is always a joy to return to the home of his parents and the care of a loving mother, he misses her cooking now that he lives alone in his own tipi. This is all possible because Wachiwi (dancing girl), who after the death of her parents, now lives with his father, Chief Matoskah, and Winona (first born daughter) his mother and Wachiwi is spending the night with her best friend Kimimila (butterfly) and her new family in their tipi. Lucky for him to spend the night warm and loved and now, early meal is served. Fortune has smiled on him as he has his warm early meal, served by his mother who dotes over him like a young boy child.

Chief Matoskah is awake and asks for a full accounting of his trip to meet Chief Bagwungijik. Wanagiyata tells his story and how he is thankful that Wakantanka (God) gave him the healing powers to help Chief Bagwungijik's paralyzed daughter Gidagaakoons (fawn - Chippewa dialect). She had a broken back from a fall and was in great pain, but no more does she suffer and walks among her people as before, all due to Wakantanka's power of healing through Wanagiyata hand. Chief Matoskah is very impressed and says he will call the tribe together tonight and give a story-telling of his son and his way of being wawakankan (one who does wonderful things – Lakota dialect) and the kindness shown on his mission to meet with the Chippewa. Then all will feast and many will perform the Wiwanyank Wacipi (the Sundance) and sign and chant long into the night.

Wanagiyata is looking forward to the night's celebration, not for the praise of his father, Chief Matoskah, to the village people, although he is somewhat embarrassed, he is thankful his father honors him in such a way of showing recognition to the Oglala Lakota people he leads. His main anticipation is to see the beautiful maiden, Wachiwi, dance in her most graceful form of storytelling movement. He has missed her greatly and has been reminded of this as he witnessed Luzahan (swift) his brother brave's newly formed feelings of affection for the Chippewa maiden, Fawn (Gidagaakoons - Chippewa dialect), the daughter of Chief Bagwungijik.

Luzahan had cared for her when he remained in the Chippewa camp while Wanagiyata was being summoned from his Oglala Lakota village. The two young ones from other tribal cultures have bonded, even though they did not speak each other's dialect. This bond was created by kindness and selfless attention by Luzahan in his daily attention and care to Fawn while she was paralyzed with her broken back and in severe pain.

All the Oglala Lakota villagers are proud of the mission of mercy Wanagiyata has completed, increasing the trust between the Chippewa village of Chief Bagwungijik and their tribal members. It is good to have allies instead of enemies and the future of this alliance could grow even stronger, as friendships blossoms between tribal members. When Chief Matoskah has finished his story telling, all the villagers come around Wanagiyata and touch him in a sign of respect.

Now the time for the Sundance has arrived and Wanagiyata will see Wachiwi dance and he will be all eyes as she dances in harmony with the drum beats. She catches the eyes of Wanagiyata following her as she moves around the great campfire, dancing her very best, hoping to please him with her talented movements and graceful display of her gifts she has honed to perfection and truly earned her name of Dancing Girl.

She smiles whenever she sees him looking at her. He has been hearing a lot of praise for her, from his mother, for Wachiwi has been a big help to his mother and his father, and they have grown to love her as their own daughter and that is good to have such joy among this family, as Wanagiyata is now out of the nest.

Time will tell more stories about this family, but not just yet, because Chief Matoskah has told his son another story, a story that concerns him. While Wanagiyata has been gone to the Chippewa village on his mission of mercy, his father has reported to him earlier in the day that there has been trouble. The trouble was that while some of the Oglala Lakota braves were on a hunt for tatanka, when a hunting party of Pawnee from the Wašín (fat not dried out – Lakota dialect) Wakpá (River – Lakota dialect) —South Platte River area of present day Nebraska now living in Oklahoma— had ventured into the Oglala Lakota hunting grounds. They had taken many tatanka before the Oglala Lakota could hunt them for their village.

The Oglala Lakota hunting party were greatly outnumbered and were forced to stay out of sight and came back to the village empty-handed and have asked Chief Matoskah to teach the Pawnee a lesson that they cannot hunt in Oglala Lakota lands. Chief Matoskah is ready to mount a raid against the Pawnee Nation, who are enemies of the Oglala Lakota. But first he must know their strength in numbers and locate the village of those, who have hunted on Oglala Lakota land.

Chief Matoskah asked his son to join him in his tipi or owoglake (a council chamber to consult or confer – Lakota dialect). "My son, I must ask you to go and find the Pawnee offenders, who take our food without asking for permission to hunt upon our hunting grounds. They have taken food from our

44

young and our elders suffer and that is bad to bear. The old and the young must not suffer hunger, because we do not defend what has been given to us by Mother Earth. The blood of our ancestors must not be wasted, who have defended our lands in times long past."

Chief Matoskah had in his mind to go and find the Pawnee hunters and punish them. "Now, I ask you, son, to scout them and find their wowaš'ake (strength – Lakota dialect) in numbers and the best way to takpe (to come upon, attack – Lakota dialect) their village? Take Luzahan and Ciqala (little one) and go with extra šunkawakans (a horse) on tomorrow's sun with my blessing," says Chief Matoskah. "I will go in an early sunrise and do as you have asked in council, my father," responds Wanagiyata.

He has wanted to spend more time at the village and spend some time with Wachiwi, as he has grown to have deep feelings for her. However his newly assigned mission carries a very important objective and he must not tarry (to delay or be tardy in acting or doing – English language) or be šuška (tardy – Lakota dialect) in his duty to his people and their welfare and his chief's request.

A mid-morning sun finds Wanagiyata, Luzahan and Ciqala, along with Šungmanitu (a wolf) Aitancan (the ruler over) and two of his best šungmanitu scouts, who run in front as point scouts as they hunt for the Pawnee hunters. The mission is under way at a trotting pace with extra horses and šungmanitu scouts moving with determination as they close the distance to their tatanka hunting grounds.

Three days ride on horseback have placed the Oglala Lakota scouts in the area of the killing of buffalo by the Pawnee. Signs

45

of the hunt's success by the Pawnee are found and are not so cold as to fool the scent's message deep within the nostrils of Šungmanitu Ruler and his two wolf scouts. They begin to track the scent of the Pawnee hunters with their three Oglala Lakota brothers, following on horseback close behind.

Šungmanitu Ruler is flanked on each side by his wolf scouts

as they track the Pawnee hunters. His keen sense of smell tells him, they are gaining on the Pawnee hunters and they should find them within a day and a half. The Pawnee hunters are on foot and carrying stolen tatanka meat and cannot move faster than those, who hunt them down on horseback.

Šungmanitu Ruler has been running far ahead of Wanagiyata, Luzahan, and Ciqala and Wolf Ruler spots the Pawnee hunters and slows to wait for his brothers of the Oglala Lakota to reach him. Sign language from Šungmanitu Ruler's tail movements and stance, tells Wanagiyata what he wants to know.

Now the Oglala Lakota braves mission becomes a silent scouting of the Pawnee hunters as they draw near to their village. Wanagiyata holds back some distance from the Pawnee village as the Pawnee hunters enter their village. He sends Luzahan on foot along with Wolf Ruler, to scout the village and number the Pawnee warriors. They return swiftly with that number and he scouts the landscape and plans the best area to launch an attack upon this toka (enemy – Lakota dialect) who steal their food.

The news from Luzahan upon his return reports the toka numbers in kicamnayan (in an overwhelming way – Lakota dialect). It appears Wanagiyata's entire Oglala Lakota village does not have enough warriors to defeat these Pawnee enemies, and he must go back to his father, Chief Matoskah, and report the scouting results to him.

In the meantime, Wanagiyata will go to Wakantanka in prayer when he returns and ask for advice and knowledge in a plan of action to keep the Pawnee from Oglala Lakota hunting grounds. He prays, also that the Pawnee will not find out the weakness in numbers of the Oglala Lakota village, if the Pawnee had this knowledge, their hunting grounds could be taken away from them, along with their entire village. The Pawnee custom is making slaves of those who would not die in the blood bath of war by their overwhelming numbers.

He has brought bad news and he sees his father is deeply troubled and fearful for his village's safety, so Wanagiyata goes to his favorite place where he fishes, in order to pray alone to Wakantanka for wisdom and guidance to punish the Pawnee for

stealing tatanka from his people, the main source of their food, clothing and shelter source. They must be stopped, but how, when they are so strong kicamnayan in superior numbers, he thinks to himself.

Wanagiyata will stay for two days in this place of peaceful voices, beside the gentle sounds of the river's rushing waters as they move over and around many bright colored rocks on their way to the ocean far in the distance where the sun falls each day. A place he loves blessed by Mother Earth's creatures of the wing and walkers upon the earth who talk the talk of their existence to echo among the trees where they call in the night in this magical home place they, all share. This great song, a mix of nature's creatures and natural things made by Wakantanka's love for us, and they will accompany Wanagiyata's words upward to his Creator, in the hope his words will be pleasingly considered in his request for guidance and assurance to save his beloved Oglala Lakota people.

After two days of fasting and prayer, Wanagiyata has had a great dream, an answer to his prayers from Wakantanka have been given and he makes his way home to his father's tipi, with the news of his dream. Chief Matoskah asked his son, "My son, you have gone to walk among those in the spirit land, what is your council"? Wanagiyata responds slowly with reverence, as he relates the dream he has had and the answer to his prayers to Wakantanka, "My father on my last night of prayer, my sleep was visited by a ogligle wakan (a good angel – Lakota dialect), who led me to the Chippewa village of Chief Bagwungijik, where I told him of our plan aigluhomni (to turn on, to throw one's self at, as in battle – Lakota dialect) with the Pawnee hunters and the great chief agreed to help us with many of his warriors and would come to our village iyehan (at the appointed time – Lakota dialect) of ten moons.

"The good angel then led me to the Crow village of my friend, the powerful Axxaashe (sun – Crow dialect) Bachhee (man – Crow dialect). Sun Man was very glad to see me, as I am his dear Oglala Lakota brother, and agrees to gather all his greatest warriors to help go against the Pawnee who have wronged the Oglala Lakota. He will wait for me and my Oglala

Lakota warriors, also the Chippewa warriors, to join with his warriors at his Crow village, all will go against the Pawnee under my leadership."

Chief Matoskah is very impressed by hearing of his son's dream and believes it is in fact council from Wakantanka and instructs his son to go swiftly to visit Chief Bagwungijik and Sun Man and see if they will gather together to war upon the Pawnee and keep them in their own lands. Wanagiyata readily agrees to his father's orders. He plans to leave on his recruitment mission to form a formidable force of united Indian tribes within two days, needing some rest before beginning his long journey. He also, plans to take Luzahan and Ciqala with him and Wolf Ruler as a forward scout, along with extra horses as has become his custom when okanšniyan (having no time – Lakota dialect) to waste in completing a mission of such importance.

The small group of Oglala Lakota young braves are riding at a good even pace upon their šunkawakans (horses), with Šungmanitu Ruler running ahead on point with his two most trusted šungmanitu pack members running out on each flank for added security as they head for the Chippewa village of Chief Bagwungijik. One of the mission members has an additional reason other than the mission's successful results, than the others and that is to once again see Gidagaakoons, Chief Bagwungijik's daughter.

Luzahan has been thinking about her ever since he left her side some time ago. He is wondering if she has been carrying him in her mind, as he has her. He will know when he looks into her eyes. He has her gift of a small white feather from a male Bobwhite quail feather on a deerskin string near his heart and wears it proudly for all to see, but few know its full story.

49

Wanagiyata and his charges arrive mid-afternoon at the Chippewa village and are greeted with a great welcome by all the villagers as they enter to be greeted by Chief Bagwungijik, who invites his friend into his tipi. Luzahan and Ciqala tie up all horses and feed and water them, before they go with Luzahan's friend Ma'iingan (timber wolf – Chippewa dialect) and the brother of Gidagaakoons to his wigwam (wigwam a small cone-shaped house) to rest and talk before the village celebrates their arrival.

Chief Bagwungijik listens to Wanagiyata's story and agrees and welcomes the help to punish the Pawnee, because they have killed some of his people just one cycle of the moon ago, as they were hunting upon their own hunting grounds. Chief Bagwungijik was not able to go against the entire Pawnee village who are responsible for this crime against his people, but now the opportunity to punish them is at hand.

The fact that the Pawnee are pushing into other lands and may soon be coming to his village or hunting grounds again and attack them in greater numbers, is a real fear and so he agrees with the wishes of his tribe to come against them by joining with

the Oglala Lakota braves. Chief Bagwungijik states he can bring about fifty warriors and will meet in the Oglala Lakota village in ten days.

After his council with Wanagiyata, he steps out of his tipi and calls the villagers together and orders them to provide food and lodging for their guests and celebrate honoring them. Gidagaakoons has been listening to Wanagiyata's story by her mother's side in silence, but now she helps the village women while keeping her feelings in check. She will be with Luzahan soon, as they will most certainly be together soon for campfire cooked buffalo and elk meat, along with corn and beans with sweet hogleglega (the grass pike or perhaps also, the rainbow fish) pieces.

Luzahan is seated by Wanagiyata's side with Ciqala on his other side, when Gidagaakoons serves him a clay bowl with hot tatanka and hehaka (the male elk – Lakota dialect) meat in a stewed broth and a smaller clay cup of corn and fish. She serves the first dish very slowly as she looks at him, when he looks up from the food he has been served. She now locks on to his eyes and a warm feeling goes through her body and she is frozen in her tracks for a short time, before she can hand the second cup of food to him. He also, has fixed his eyes on her beauty and knows instantly, that she is very happy to see him and he almost drops the second dish of food she has tried to hand him.

Wanagiyata has been watching this reunion with great

interest and accidently snickers and then coughs to cover up his reaction, hoping he has not embarrassed them. He feels they may become each one, a part of another tribe. He is reminded of his own feelings for Dancing Girl, Wachiwi. He pulls her from his mind to thoughts of his next part of his mission, and that is to enlist his Crow brother, a man of great strength, who he saved in his first battle with the Jicarilla Apache (see appendix page 214). He will leave in the morning when the sun breaks to light his way.

Luzahan has finished eating and gets up from his place next to Wanagiyata and slowly walks back by Ma'iingan wigwam. Gidagaakoons looks around to where Luzahan has been seated and notices he has walked away. She moves away from the dancing by a large fire and quietly moves slowly away when she sees Luzahan standing alone by her brother's wigwam. She will need Wanagiyata to interpret for her, so she goes and stands behind him for a minute and then Wanagiyata turns his head and sees her and she makes napeonwoglaka (to use the sign language – Lakota dialect), for him to follow her.

He joins her as she walks up and faces Luzahan and says, "Luzahan it is good that you are here among my people and standing before me. Your image has been in my mind and your kindness you gave me; I carry in my heart, for it is mine alone to keep." Wanagiyata repeats her words. Luzahan is honored by her open speaking of words he has hoped to hear and responds, "I know we are from different oyate (a people, nation or tribe) and that may be a mountain you cannot climb, but you need to know I have carried you in my heart when last I saw you and I can see no other maidens face, only yours. If your father would give his blessing, I would bring him horses to take your hand in marriage, if that is also your desire"?

Again, Wanagiyata interprets Luzahan's words. Fawn is overwhelmed by these words and is silent for a moment looking into Luzahan's eyes. "Fawn takes Luzahan's hands in her hands and says, "You have had my heart when I first saw your kindness when I could not walk. I will wait for you as long as you need to bring horses to my father's care. Will you ask for my hand before you leave, so I may know if we will climb the mountain of kitanyankel (with the greatest difficulty – Lakota dialect) by separate customs together hand in hand. Wanagiyata relates Fawn's words to Luzahan and he himself is moved by them.

Luzahan nods his head in a sign of yes; he will speak to her father, Chief Bagwungijik. He will need Wanagiyata to interpret for him and ask him to do so later that night. Wanagiyata and Luzahan go and sit by the chief, who is not surprised by Luzahan's request, and in fact, seems pleased. He states, he will speak with his wife about her wishes in this matter tonight and let Luzahan know his answer. Luzahan is informed of what Chief Bagwungijik's response was to Wanagiyata and he is tokekekel (with ripe concernedness – Lakota dialect) as he awaits an answer, but it is difficult to hide any emotions to that effect that could show on his face before Wanagiyata and Chief Bagwungijik during the celebration.

Chief Bagwungijik goes to his wife's side and pulls her toward their tipi and they enter for a short time. The chief leaves his wife in the tipi and goes to Luzahan and Wanagiyata who are standing alone talking. Chief Bagwungijik looks at Luzahan and speaks to Wanagiyata, "Fawn's mother and I would be pleased to have young Luzahan as our son, if he can bring four horses to me and four buffalo tahalo (a hide – Lakota dialect) this marriage will be done and this is my will." When Wanagiyata looks at Luzahan, he quickly asks, "What did Chief Bagwungijik say"?

53

Wanagiyata answers in humorous manner, "I don't know what is blocking their eyes, it must be the great sun reflecting off the snow blinding their judgment, but they want you as *family*."

After Wanagiyata sneakers, he continues, "You must bring four šunkawakans (a horse) and four tatanka hides, when you are ready to take Fawn in marriage." Luzahan faces Chief Bagwungijik smiling and nodding in respect of his approval to marry his daughter Fawn. Luzahan finds Fawn and in sign language lets her know her parents have approved their request for marriage. No date will be set; Luzahan will come with horses and hides, when he is free to do so, as she is told by Wanagiyata before they leave in the morning.

The small party of Oglala Lakota warriors leaves on their horses, with spare horses being led close behind with Šungmanitu Ruler scouting in the lead. Sunrise finds the small band heading for the Crow village three days ride from the Chippewa village of Chief Bagwungijik. Wanagiyata's plan to go to war with the Pawnee is taking shape. He has the pledge of Chief Bagwungijik to join with him in this war effort and if he can persuade his friend the mighty warrior of the Crow, Sun Man, to join in with the Oglala Lakota and the Chippewa and, he believes united, they can defeat the Pawnee thieves.

The Crow village guard recognized Wanagiyata as he led the small band of Oglala Lakota toward his village and alerted the village of the entrance of friendly visitors. The Crow village comes alive with everyone coming to meet them, including Sun Man and Chief Chogan (blackbird – Algonquin dialect). Wanagiyata dismounts and greets his dear friend and they disappear into his tipi for council. While the friends talk, Luzahan and Ciqala are tending their horses. When Sun Man

54

comes out of his tent with Wanagiyata, he has a look of determination written across his face. The Chief Chogan calls the Elders together for a council meeting. It takes very little time, before the Elders agree that Sun Man the Crow will join the Oglala Lakota and Chippewa to go to war against the Pawnee, but first they will honor their special guest with food and dancing in celebration, along with sheltering them for the night. The plan is for Sun Man to remain in his village and ready his warriors for battle and wait for Wanagiyata and Chief Bagwungijik to join him and together they will go against the large Pawnee village.

Wanagiyata, Luzahan and Ciqala return to their village and begin to prepare weapons and make all ready for a war mission. Meanwhile Wanagiyata spends many hours in prayer to Wakantanka, asking for wisdom and strength, to lead in the upcoming war with the Pawnee, he also spends some time with Wachiwi walking by the talking waters of their nearby village. Wanagiyata keeps their talks about anything, that is not finalizing his need to ask for her hand in marriage, as he feels he cannot commit to this union, when he is about to go to war and may not return.

Asking for Wachiwi's hand in marriage is heavy on Wanagiyata's mind, but timing for this marriage is not possible, with everything upon his mind for his responsibility is great and he must ready himself to carry this burden well, for many lives depend upon his leadership. Wachiwi's parents have "walked on" to Mahpiya (Heaven – Lakota dialect) and now Chief Matoskah is her adopted father and guardian. Wanagiyata knows he can get his father's approval for giving Wachiwi's hand in marriage; however the time is not right for young love to take on the challenges of becoming a family. Time will dictate this union of young love, but for this time in Wanagiyata's life, it is his responsibility to lead a large number of braves to war.

The great red sun is sinking in the western sky, when Chief Bagwungijik and his war party of fifty warriors arrive at the Oglala Lakota village and are warmly greeted by Chief Matoskah and Wanagiyata. All the village is alive with a warm welcome and a huge fire, which has rapidly been constructed and food is abundantly served for all the guest Chippewa braves. Wanagiyata lays out his plan of attack to Chief Bagwungijik and he passes this battle plan out to his braves. The combined war party of one hundred Oglala Lakota and Chippewa braves rest and prepare themselves for battle using war paint and more time for making more arrows and spears, before heading out to the village of Sun Man.

The Oglala Lakota ride their horses and bring spares horses, who now carry some of the Chippewa braves, being led by the Oglala Lakota braves. The Chippewa braves are rotated so some will get to rest riding on the Oglala Lakota spare horses, while the others walk. This practice saves the Chippewa braves some hardship in the travel to the Crow village. They will rest at the Crow village, before heading out to battle the Pawnee, days away.

Sun Man welcomes his friend, Wanagiyata, and is introduced

to Chief Bagwungijik by Wanagiyata, who speaks all three dialects, his great gift from Wakantanka. The battle plan is laid out before Sun Man at this time. The Chippewa on horseback will hide in the trees out of sight of the Pawnee village. Meanwhile, Chief

Bagwungijik will take fifty of his braves who are on foot and attacks from the eastern side of the Pawnee village. This will put the sun at their backs and the sun directly in the eyes of the defending Pawnee braves, who will rush to defend their village.

This action will draw the Pawnee defending warriors out from the village and then the Chippewa will retreat, allowing Wanagiyata and his braves on horseback to run in between the Pawnee warriors and their village. This action will cut them off from their village and then Chief Bagwungijik and his Chippewa braves will turn and attack the Pawnee. Sun Man and his one hundred and fifty warriors will come in from the north and south, half from each side. This will give Sun Man seventy five warriors coming in from each direction, all closing in on the Pawnee forces. The enemy number is about six hundred Pawnee braves, being attacked from all sides by Wanagiyata's and his combination of warriors.

The Pawnee well outnumber the Oglala Lakota, Chippewa and Crow braves by more than two to one, but the element of surprise will leave the Pawnee not fully prepared for war, with limited arrows and spears at the ready, they are ill-prepared for a full out battle. It is a good battle plan and will be followed by all, as agreed. Wanagiyata will wait with his warriors on horseback for Chief Bagwungijik to begin the fighting, drawing the Pawnee out of their village, while Sun Man will lead his warriors and unleash his awesome power upon the enemy Pawnee, the likes of which they have never seen before. It is zuya (war – Lakota dialect).

Wanagiyata leads his mix of tribal warriors to a location near the Pawnee village and the warriors all take their positions and ready themselves to takpe (to come upon, attack), just before sunrise. Chief Bagwungijik waits for the sun to rise at his back and gives the signal to attack. The Pawnee guards now sound the alarm and all the Pawnee villager braves grab the weapons they can and hurry out to meet the attacking Chippewa.

Chief Bagwungijik runs in front of his warriors and bravely meets two braves with tomahawks. He shoots one with his bow, placing his arrow directly into his heart. The second brave bears swiftly down on him and receives a spear in the stomach, but the Pawnee brave wounds Chief Bagwungijik in the left shoulder with a deep cut from his tomahawk before he goes down doubled up in pain as his life drains slowly away. Chief Bagwungijik falls back behind his braves and gives the command to retreat. The Chippewa warriors all turn and run away with the Pawnee braves giving chase.

Wanagiyata and his mounted warriors move their horses in behind the Pawnee and attack them from the rear, now they have stopped chasing the Chippewa braves and turn to face this new threat bearing down upon them. Luzahan and Ciqala ride side by side in the attack and each use their spears on two Pawnee braves with tomahawks. Now they use their bows and bring down more Pawnee warriors. They have retreated in a circle and fix arrows for another shot into the Pawnee braves; each arrow finds its killing mark.

As the Pawnee turn to fight the Oglala Lakota riders, the Chippewa braves turn around and begin to fight with the Pawnee and now Sun Man and his Crow braves attack from the north and south.

Sun Man uses his large wicat'e (an instrument with which to kill – Lakota dialect), consisting of a large heavy stone affixed to a strong wooden handle, that no one else could use, but him in battle because of its heavy weight. But in his powerful right arm, it is a very formidable weapon.

When Sun Man moves in on the Pawnee, he goes through them like he is swatting flies. Soon Wanagiyata comes face to face with the Pawnee Chief Bear (kuúruks – Pawnee dialect) Claw (aspiitu' – Pawnee dialect) who has pulled him off his horse from behind and they are in a hand to hand battle with their knives. The Pawnee Chief is strong and puts up a good fight, but Wanagiyata cuts his right forearm very deeply with a swipe of his sharp flint knife and the chief drops his knife and his face shows that he is awaiting his fate. Wanagiyata grabs him by the neck and tells him in Pawnee dialect to tell his brave to surrender.

All fighting stops as Wanagiyata shouts out in all different dialects, the order to stop fighting in Oglala Lakota, Crow and Chippewa. All fighting has stopped and all the Pawnee braves are herded together and surrounded by the Oglala Lakota, Chippewa and Crow warriors. There are many wounded and many more dead on both sides, but mostly the Pawnee losses are much heavier.

Wanagiyata orders all the wounded to be moved into the Pawnee village and makes sure there are no other braves to fight. All the Pawnee women, young and old are afraid, but Wanagiyata tells them to be calm and then he goes to all the wounded Oglala Lakota, Chippewa, including Chief Bagwungijik, and all Crow warriors who are wounded and heals them, then he heals all the wounded Pawnee braves and saves the

Pawnee chief for last.

The entire Pawnee villagers along with their warriors drop to their knees and raise their arms high toward the sky, as if to praise the Creator, Wakantanka. Wanagiyata speaks directly to The Pawnee chief, "Do not come against the Oglala Lakota, Chippewa, and Crow, do not hunt upon their lands without their honoring of the hunt. Do you hear the words I have spoken"? The Pawnee chief, realizing, he may be able to see another sunrise, shakes his head in a sign of agreement.

Luzahan and Ciqala along with other Oglala Lakota braves have been rounding up all the old villagers, along with the young and all the women. They are brought to hear Wanagiyata's words and are very fearful about being killed or taken into slavery, as is the custom of most Indian tribes of the time. Wanagiyata speaks again, "We are peaceful people, but your hunters have stolen food from our hunting grounds and even killed some of the Chippewa tribal members and that is why we have brought war upon your village. Wakantanka has healed your wounded through me and has called for mercy on all remaining here among your tribe. His Wish is to take no prisoners, as slaves, and go in peace, if your chief agrees to become a friend to the Oglala Lakota, Chippewa and Crow Nations."

Looking at the Pawnee chief, on his knees, the chief is

showing the look of relief on his weathered face and speaks up, "Your words of friendship, your actions, speak out mercy, to the Pawnee; it shall be as you have spoken. We will be a friend to all who have come here to war

60

against us, but we part in friendship. We thank Wakantanka for His mercy, His healing powers, for all wounded here as myself."

All Oglala Lakota, Chippewa, and Crow warriors killed in battle are placed on the spare horses and leave the Pawnee village and head for their own villages. The battle was very one sided and the losses of thirty four braves among the three tribes was light compared to the Pawnee, who lost over two hundred braves, due mostly to Sun Man and his great strength, as he alone killed over one hundred braves with his mighty arm and heavy wicat'e. His great strength will be told in many stories by the Pawnee as they will respect their new friends and the healing power of Wakantanka through the person of Wanagiyata

Until our next Campfire Story Telling – "Returning Warriors," may Wakantanka be with you.

Tipi in the snow

Chapter 4

Returning Warriors

In the aftermath of the great battle between the attacking Oglala Lakota, Chippewa and Crow against the Pawnee Indians, all the attacking tribes gathered up their dead, and wrapped them in tatanka (a male buffalo) robes, given to them by the defeated Pawnee. The Oglala Lakota losses were five braves, the Chippewa losses were seventeen and the Crow suffered twelve warriors killed. All the dead were loaded on the Oglala Lakota horses and the three tribes left the Pawnee village in the late morning. Wanagiyata (in the land of spirits), Chief Bagwungijik (hole in the sky – Chippewa dialect) and Axxaashe (sun – Crow dialect) Bachhee (man – Crow dialect), Sun Man's warriors would be placed high in trees tied to their large tree branches. They are all grouped together in nearby trees as their souls headed to Mahpiya (Heaven, the clouds, the afterlife of mankind). Together they fought and died, together their bodies would sleep in the trees away from the šungmanitus (wolves – Lakota dialect) and šunkmanitus (coyotes – Lakota dialect) closer to their journey high above the stars. All was solemn when the last of the dead were placed high in the trees, and Wanagiyata prayed for the dead. Wanagiyata had already cut a lock of hair from each brave who had "walked on" to take back to his relatives for the grieving ceremony, as is the Oglala Lakota custom.

A day's travel from the burial grounds of their brothers, camp was made and all the Oglala Lakota, Chippewa and Crow warriors celebrated their great victory in battle and gave thanks  to Wakantanka (God) that the threat of the Pawnee upon their villages would be no more. The hunting grounds would once again be able to feed their people and provide clothing and shelter when the cold of winter makes a visit each year on all living things with its wind-blown sting. This is a time to shelter in a tatanka hide covered tipi (teepee, or tent, or lodge) and eat the food they have gathered in the season of plenty.

Sun Man and his braves bid Wanagiyata and Chief Bagwungijik a farewell and each head for their village, with the promise to meet for a powwow (a North American Indian gathering ceremony involving feasting, singing, dancing, and trading) in the next early spring after the ice has turned to water and the green buds begin to sprout upon the tree limbs as new life shows her colors. The powwow will be near the village of the Oglala Lakota. Chief Bagwungijik agreed to bring his tribe of Chippewa to the powwow, where trading among the tribes would take place, along with the shared celebrations of each tribe's culture being displayed to enhance friendly tribal relations in the future.

Luzahan (swift) bid Chief Bagwungijik a farewell with the help of Wanagiyata, to interpret his words in Chippewa. He had already asked for the hand of Gidagaakoons (fawn - Chippewa dialect) in marriage telling him, he would have the payment of four horses and four tatanka hides soon. He also asked, if the wedding could take place at the powwow in the early spring. Chief Bagwungijik readily agreed and headed to his village with a great joy in his heart, for he had grown very fond of Luzahan and welcomed the idea of having two sons to call his own and he would soon have grandsons, if nature's way would be followed faithfully.

Sun Man and his Crow warriors reached their village and the wailing of wives and families began for those who were lost in battle. A time of mourning would continue for two days and then

 day three all the Crow villagers would celebrate the great victory over the Pawnee village.

Many stories were told by the various braves that saw the awesome power of their great warrior, Sun Man, as he slew over a hundred Pawnee warriors. Even now the Pawnee

villagers were telling stories of this mighty Crow warrior. These stories would spread to other villages among the Pawnee Nation. Wanagiyata's healing powers would also be spoken of, with great reverence and this word of his healing would spread rapidly.

After Wanagiyata reaches his Oglala Lakota village, he bids his faithful Šungmanitu (a wolf) Aitancan (the ruler over) and his two wolf scouts a farewell and gives them as much tatanka meat that they could eat in a way of thanking them for their service to him. Šungmanitu Ruler brushes the legs of Wanagiyata twice with his head and then the full length on his hard body and then leads his two šungmanitu scouts off into the forest to join his main šungmanitu pack, who have missed their leader and his ability to hunt for prey with his keen nose and knowledge of the ways of the wild things. Šungmanitu Ruler's leadership would soon begin ayuhlagan (to make large upon – Lakota dialect) each one's ikpi (belly – Lakota dialect) with fresh meat.

Wanagiyata and his warriors are exhausted from their long journey before they reach their Oglala Lakota village in the late afternoon. Once again mourning takes place by the families of the lost warriors and the crying and chanting sounds of sorrow fill the air, as the returning Oglala Lakota file into the village and the toll of those returning is realized by the missing warriors who are silently named.

Chief Matoskah (white bear) and Winona (first born daughter) greet their son in silence, but with a thankful heart that Wakantanka has spared their son. Wachiwi (dancing girl) comes out of the chief's tipi and her face lights up like a twinkling star on a black night's sky, at the sight of Wanagiyata. She has been very worried about his safety, along with Winona his mother, as the two work together to make a good life for Chief Matoskah the head of their family and the wise chief of the Oglala Lakota.

The two Oglala Lakota women have bonded like mother and daughter since Wachiwi came to live with Chief Matoskah and Winona after her parents were killed by a renegade Chippewa raider and have grown to share a great love for one another. The two Oglala Lakota women both love Wanagiyata, however, one kind of love is a mother's love and the other is a truly romantic love, which is all consuming.

Chief Matoskah invites his son to talk the talk of his mission. Wanagiyata signs for them to go to his empty tipi, where they can talk in privacy. Wanagiyata begins his detailed story telling as his father, who is seated on a tatanka hide, across from his son. Chief Matoskah is very proud of his son who has special talents in healing and leadership and walks among the spirits in spirit land, all within his dreams.

The great Oglala Lakota chief is very pleased by the great deeds his son has accomplished and how he has led the great battle against the Pawnee. Even more, that he changed the once toka (one of a foreign or hostile nation, an enemy) Pawnee, into this one Pawnee village of dakotas (allies or friends) through his act of mercy and healing. While Wanagiyata is story-telling to his father, he brings up the idea he has developed to keep the friendly tribes together as dakotas. "My father, I have invited the Crow and Chippewa villagers to rendezvous here in early spring. What I am asking would be a risk, as the Pawnee Nation has over one hundred and fifty villages and is a very powerful enemy nation to many tribes, including the Oglala Lakota Nation.

"I am asking your council on the wisdom of inviting the Pawnee villagers that we have conquered, to join us at this year's powwow, as a sign of friendship and a time of trading. Also, I am thinking about inviting Chief Cougar (Ndolkan – Jicarilla Apache dialect) Man (Homme – Jicarilla Apache dialect), Cougar Man and his Jicarilla Apache (see appendix page 214) villagers to attend as a show of faith through friendship. What are your words of council my father"?

Chief Matoskah answers, "I feel with our combined numbers of Chippewa, Crow, and now the village of Pawnee you conquered is our dakotas, that if the Pawnee come, it will be in peace. Who will you send to the Pawnee with this invitation to come to our powwow"? "I will think on your words my father; my answer will come soon," Wanagiyata pauses.

"There is one more request my father, I wish to ask for the hand of Wachiwi in marriage and would like the marriage to be held during the powwow with your blessing and that of my dear mother. Also, my friend Luzahan has asked wakanyuza (to take a wife – Lakota dialect), the Chippewa daughter of Chief Bagwungijik. He asks for her to be tawicu (his wife – Lakota dialect) and would also like to tawicuwaton (to be married – Lakota dialect) at the powwow. What are your words"? asks Wanagiyata. Chief Matoskah responds saying, "I will speak with your mother this night and think of what I will ask for Wachiwi's hand, as I am her titakuye (immediate relatives) now. I will come to your tipi in the morning with my words."

The night passes slowly and still there are sounds of mourning, although they are softer in tone and many do not sleep and Wanagiyata is counted among them, thinking of all his mission has accomplished along with thoughts of having his parent's blessing to winyancin (to buy a wife – Lakota dialect), that being Wachiwi.

This leaves Ciqala (little one) as the only single one among the three young Oglala Lakota braves bound in deep friendship, but that should not last long, as he has his eye on a tall maiden. She seems to favor him more as his stature grows in respect among the tribal members. In spite of his short stature, he has great stature among his tribe and is a big part of the great stories told by Wanagiyata and Luzahan.

Wanagiyata was up early as the medicine man has started the two-day mourning funeral ritual for the five Oglala Lakota warriors who have "walked on" to the spirit land. During these next days of funeral rites he will attend the funeral for two days and one night. Only a true medicine man or a highly respected woman with a high status can provide this funeral in a respectful manner. Grief is expressed by crying, wailing, chanting and singing, along with cutting of hair and even cutting on one's body.

There are Seven Sacred Ceremonies of the Pipe. One of these is Nagi (the soul or spirit – Lakota dialect) Gluha (to have or possess one's own – Lakota dialect) 'Keeping of the Soul', which is meant to purify the soul of the one who "walked on." This rite helps them to go to the place they were born.

A lock of hair, which Wanagiyata collected from each warrior lost, is held above burning sweetgrass to help purify it, then it is placed in a piece of sacred deerskin from the medicine man. The deerskin is called a 'soul bundle'. A sacred pipe is smoked and a relative then places the 'soul bundle' in their tipi. The keeper of the 'soul bundle' must vow to live a harmonious life until the soul can be released from the 'soul bundle' when it is taken outside the tipi and let fly into the wind, usually in one year's time.

If the "Keeper of the Soul" judged this person a person of value, the hair —representing the soul— would be released to the right and would fly on to Wakantanka. In this case, the hair was all to be released, as no body ashes were brought back from the special warriors united in burial among the high limbs of trees, chosen by Wanagiyata, Chippewa Chief Bagwungijik and Sun Man of the Crow. These times of mourning brought all the villagers closer together as they grieved as one family.

The three Oglala Lakota braves know the truth that the only way to Mahpiya (Heaven), is to believe in Wakantanka and His Son, Wanikiye (the Savior – Lakota dialect), known to the Indian Nations as Tatanka Ska Son in the form of a white buffalo. The Oglala Lakota tribe is learning more about how to be assured that they will be with Wakantanka from the three 'Story Tellers'. However, the old custom has some good lessons of good clean living and is a good way to mourn for family and friends of those who have "walked on."

Before Wanagiyata left his tipi to join the mourning of those lost in battle, Chief Matoskah enters after announcing his presence. "My son, I have good news, your mother and I give our blessing to your marriage to be performed at powwow. I approve of Luzahan's marriage to Chief Bagwungijik's daughter this spring. I require five horses and five tatanka ha ((buffalo skin or hide with hair – Lakota dialect). That is a price of respect for Wachiwi, my sweet dancing girl," states Chief Matoskah.

"It shall be done my father and I thank you and my dear mother for your blessing of Wachiwi. I will ask Wachiwi for her hand after all mourning ceremony ends," states Wanagiyata. "Wise words I hear my son, you may invite the Pawnee, but have one of the Pawnee go to Chief Cougar Man and pass my words, that they are welcome to join in the powwow, come blossom time." says Chief Matoskah.

The days of mourning have gone by and it is time for Wanagiyata to go to Wachiwi and propose marriage to her. He has stayed clear of her since he returned from war with the Pawnee, because of his duty during the mourning period to the families of the fallen. This duty has had his full attention, as expected of him as the leader of the battle and he must pay homage to the families of the fallen, as is the custom of most leaders.

He goes to his family's tipi and asks for Wachiwi to come out. She comes out and is dressed in a beautiful tan deerskin dress with a necklace of bright multi-colored river shells. Her hair is braided with strips of blue and white colored deerskin entwined within the braids of her shining black hair.

She is truly beautiful, it is clear she has expected his visit and wants to look her very best, for she feels this is a special time to impress the one she loves. "Wachiwi, will you walk with me"? asked Wanagiyata. She offers her hand to him and he guides her away toward the mountain stream nearby and they begin to walk along it's bank with the sound of the water singing her song as if

 ordered to perform for the young couple on this special day, with no wind to block her song coming forth to those in love.

The two young Oglala Lakota halt their walking by a large

boulder and lean against it facing the fast water, taking in the sound of nature's melody standing hand in hand, each one waiting for words to form, but not rushing the joy of this moment. "Wachiwi, I have been long in telling you of my feelings for you, held deeply in my heart. Many challenges have been met, many missions to complete for my father. I think of you almost every moment I am still. I have asked my father and mother to take you as my bride. Is your heart standing with mine, or do I stand alone in this life? You will honor me greatly to be my bride when early spring brings the powwow to our village. I ask you now to be my love until the sun no longer shines in my eyes, when morning breaks across the high mountain and I have "walked on." Do you feel as I, and carry me in your heart, as I have carried you to many faraway places"? asks Wanagiyata.

Wanagiyata takes both of Wachiwi's hands and faces her, looking into her eyes, waiting for her to answer. "Wanagiyata, I have loved you for long before you knew I was a maiden as a very young girl. I can love no other but you. I cannot love another in my life, so live long and be my husband for all time," answers Wachiwi.

The two hold each other, as bears will sometimes hug in a playful manner and sway back and forth in pure joy. This is a moment the two Oglala Lakota youths will always remember, for it is their coming together alone speaking of their love and looking toward their spring time marriage during powwow.

Luzahan has started his journey to the Chippewa village of Chief Bagwungijik to buy his daughter Gidagaakoons his bride to be at the spring time powwow. He has brought along his good friend Ciqala and has the payment for Gidagaakoons of four horses and four tatanka hides. He is leading two and Ciqala is leading the other two very fine horses, which he hopes Chief Bagwungijik will be pleased with.

Luzahan knows it is some months until powwow and he wants to head off any possible bids against his offer to buy the beautiful Gidagaakoons. Ciqala is thinking more each day about the tall and long-legged beauty, who has caught his eye and others see her beauty as well. He is reminded that he will be all alone, while his dear brothers will be getting married soon. He is still with his parents, but that is not the same as having your own tipi and a sweet wife to care for you in the small ways, he cannot give himself.

It is cold and the snow is blowing on a horizontal pattern and Luzahan and Ciqala are pushing on at a steady pace, some three hours out from the Chippewa village and both are very cold and thinking of a warm visit and the sharing of a wigwam (wigwam a small cone-shaped house) with an arched roof made from wooden frames that were covered with sheets of birch bark and woven mats that were held in place by ropes or strips of wood. Some were covered with buffalo hides for these tribe members, who follow the tatanka herds and were constantly on the move hunting them.

Wigwams were usually round in shape —eight to ten feet tall and ten to fifteen feet wide at the bottom— and warm in the winter snows. The two were looking forward to being inside Gidagaakoons's brother, Ma'iingan's (timber wolf – Chippewa dialect), warm wigwam and share his hot food, while the sharing of friendship by a warm fire in his tatanka covered wigwam were ruling their thoughts, as the cold winds bite made it so. They decide to speed up a little more, which will also keep their horses warmer and make their trip a little shorter.

73

The sun light has been blocked by the heavy snow and darkness is almost upon them, as they break into Chief Bagwungijik's Chippewa village. The two Oglala Lakota braves are warmly welcomed. Luzahan goes to meet with Chief Bagwungijik and presents his four tatanka hides and shows the four prized horses to him before putting them under some trees for shelter. He then feeds and waters them and gives each a rubdown, before he goes with his friend Ma'iingan and the warmth of his campfire and food, which he is very pleased to be served by Gidagaakoons.

Life is good with a warm campfire, friends around you with hot food to share when it is snowing heavily with a strong howling wind to drive the cold deep into your bones. Gidagaakoons touches Luzahan's hand when she delivers hot elk meat to him in a round clay bowl. He knows he has made the right decision to choose her to be his bride, even though he also realizes the challenges they will face being from different tribes and cultures, but he will face all with a deep love for her.

Luzahan and Ciqala will sleep soundly tonight as their journey has been long and hard, with much snow in the face mixed with strong winds to sting the checks and blur the eyes. Luzahan thanks Wakantanka for their sturdy šunkawakans, which warmed their hus (legs – Lakota dialect) and ništušte (the rump – Lakota dialect) under their tatanka blankets turned with the hide side facing outward and fur side in, which also is draped far back and over their horse's rump providing more protection for them as well.

Before sleeping in his warm tatanka blanket, he thanks his Wakantanka for his safe trip and the joy he feels at this special time among another tribe, he will very soon call family. All because of his dear brother, Wanagiyata's healing powers and kindness to his future bride.

He thinks to himself about all these things, as sleep begins to claim his joyful thoughts, he will always be grateful to his dear Oglala Lakota brother Wanagiyata. He is also grateful to have Ciqala for his undying friendship and loyalty even in times of hardship or danger. Life is good and with that last thought, he drops into the deep void of a night to the healing powers of much needed sleep.

Luzahan is first to wake, as Gidagaakoons is by his side with more warm food consisting of buffalo meat, beans, corn and some squash and what looked orange in color, which he later found out was pumpkin. He received this early meal with a big smile from his future bride and then after he accepted his bowl of food, Gidagaakoons brought him, she presented him with a gift of high topped taha (a deerskin) hanpa (moccasins – Lakota dialect) and tatanka hide leggings. Which she made for him as a gift from her to him at their wedding, but she wanted him to have them for his trip back to his village in the cold winter weather, now that he was here. She would have time to make other gifts.

Gidagaakoons was wearing a beautiful buckskin dress, with a robe of buffalo hide to keep her warm. She removed her tatanka robe and sat down facing Luzahan, as he ate his early meal, smiling in silence. Luzahan smiled back at her in between bites of his hot early meal. He thought to himself, how nice this act of kindness might be each morning after they were married.

When he finished his early meal, he pulled the white feather she had given him out from the front of his deerskin shirt to show her, that he carried her gift she gave him some time after they first met. Gidagaakoons smile broadened even more upon

75

seeing the white bobtail feather she gave him. 'I carry this always and think of you often,' says Luzahan in sign language. 'When will you go?' asks Gidagaakoons in sign language. Luzahan answers her in sign, 'I must leave in two suns.'

Gidagaakoons's brother Ma'iingan wakes up and looks at his sister and smiles and she says, "I will bring your early meal and food for Ciqala now" and she leaves in a slow graceful manner and smiles back at Luzahan as she slips though the hide covered door flap, closing it behind her. Ma'iingan gets out of his warm blanket and brings the low campfire of wood coals by petkaile s'e (in the manner of fanning a fire to life by adding wood – Lakota dialect) and blowing the embers to catch the new wood he added to spring to flames and make it more comfortable as the cold night has cooled his wigwam and he wants to care for his friends Luzahan and Ciqala, now his honored guest.

Ciqala has heard the Chippewa dialect spoken between brother and sister and sits up in his tatanka blanket and rubs his eyes and says, "My brother is that food I smell"? "Your nose would make that of a šungmanitu very nawizi (to be jealous or envious – Lakota dialect)," states Luzahan. Just as Ciqala has stood up, Gidagaakoons enters the wigwam with two bowls of hot food handing one to Ciqala and the other to her brother. Ciqala signs a thank you to Gidagaakoons, and thinks to himself, how kind and caring she is. He is glad his brother, Luzahan, will have her caring love very soon and it brings to life thoughts of Kimimila (butterfly) with her slim beauty and smiling face. He wonders if she would make a wife as good as Gidagaakoons. His thoughts are now following the news his nose has brought him and he starts to eat his share of the hot stew brought to him, as he sits down on his warm buffalo blanket.

Chief Bagwungijik and his son Ma'iingan, take Ciqala fishing, while Luzahan and Gidagaakoons spend time sitting together in her father and mother's wigwam, under the watchful eye of his future mother-in-law Amitola (rainbow – Chippewa dialect). The two speak in sign language for a short time before they eat again, then Luzahan goes back to Ma'iingan's wigwam and rest some more, before Chief Bagwungijik and Ciqala return. They return with some nice trout which they will have at tonight's celebration in honor of the visiting Oglala Lakota braves.

The celebration for Luzahan and Ciqala visit is short because of the blowing snow, but there were two dances and some songs and chants in their honor and that was well received by both and would be remembered always. More 'Campfire Stories' would be told of this petileyapi (kindling – Lakota dialect) of fellowship shared between the Oglala Lakota and Chippewa people, by both tribes.

It is a cold morning in the Chippewa village when Luzahan and Ciqala bid good bye to their new friends and Luzahan and Gidagaakoons take each other's hand, as he slowly rides away on his horse and she walks alongside him for some distance before she stops and break their hand holds. She remains standing and watches as Luzahan rides away in the blowing snow and he keeps looking back at her, as her slim figure fades away, like a ghost disappearing, as if covered in snow. Luzahan, at this moment, feels for the very first time what true loneliness means after losing sight of Gidagaakoons his future bride. It will be a long winter for both he and Wanagiyata, waiting for powwow and the youthful maidens to become their wives.

The only comfort Luzahan feels on his return trip to the

Oglala Lakota village is the warmth of his new high-top taha hanpa and buffalo leggings, a gift from Gidagaakoons, which he is using well as wind-blown snow swirls all around him as he leads Ciqala forward toward home. He is truly grateful for this early gift as the winter's cold teeth bite all she can reach, who are unprepared to turn her away with proper pre-planning.

The return of Luzahan and Ciqala is a welcome sight to all the Oglala Lakota villagers, as they were aware of the mission Luzahan was on when he left to travel to the Chippewa village to buy Gidagaakoons from Chief Bagwungijik. Wanagiyata pats both his dear Oglala Lakota brothers on their shoulders and invites them into his tipi for their story telling and some hot food made by his mother Winona and Wachiwi, which would come soon.

Luzahan and Ciqala both tell their stories, eat and then take to their warm tatanka blankets and sleep is their welcome companion. It is good for them to be home and safe from the winter's storm chasing them with her teeth bared and a biting cold promise to be kept by strong winds and heavy snow.

Ciqala wakes up early and his first thought is of the maiden Kimimila. He knows he must not waste time in asking for her hand from Ciqala's father, Ḣoka (badger – Lakota dialect), now her new father she lives with and her mother, Wicahpi (star – Lakota dialect). She is loved like their own cinca (a child – Lakota dialect).

Many other braves have noticed her beauty and that she has come of age as a woman. Now that his brothers are taking a wife, he must think of doing so. He will ask Ḣoka for her hand, but first he would like to know if she has the same feelings for him.

78

Kimimila is walking to his father's tipi with some wood she has gathered in the cold among the snow-covered trees and cold blowing wind. She sees Ciqala walking toward her and she stops. Ciqala says, "Kimimila, I have been thinking of you for many moons and when my eyes are far away from you, I see you in my mind as ogligle wakan (a good angel) and still I am lonely. I ask you now; do you hold me in your heart with the care not to crush a spring flower or do you favor another among the braves of our village? I could buy you without your heart pointed at me, but that is not my way and should not be the custom among our people."

Kimimila answers, "I would be honored to serve you in marriage, for I have had your spirit to carry in my heart long before you came to free me from the evil Chippewa raider, Abooksigun (wildcat – Chippewa dialect), who killed my wakihiyece (parents – Lakota dialect). "When would you ask Ḣoka for my hand"? "This day before the moon shines on the snow, I will have the answer," answers Ciqala. "Wanagiyata and Luzahan will marry at powwow, would this be your wish also"? asks Ciqala.

Kimimila drops her arms full of broken tree limbs and takes both of Ciqala's hands and says, "I truly love you, Ciqala. You have made my heart fly among the eagles this day. I will be honored to marry at powwow." Ciqala picks up the wood and walks Kimimila back to Ḣoka's tipi and hands the load of wood to her and then kisses her forehead, then opens the tatanka hide flap of the tipi, for her to enter.

A terrible winter blizzard, a white out, has hit the Oglala Lakota village, all the šunkawakans have been herded into the cave the tribe uses for women and children's safety if attacked.

Food and water are stored there for the horses and those who are assigned to care for them. It is a blessing to have this shelter to meet the needs for the Oglala Lakota villagers. The rest of the villagers are staying inside their tipis and keep their fires from going cold. They keep a supply of wood for three days, just for emergency, and this is a good plan.

The Oglala Lakota people know how to plan for hard times, they have a good supply of smoked tatanka, elk, deer and some fish. If they need water, they melt the snow, which is now about two feet deep around the base of the tipis and mounting, as the storm rages outside their sturdy tipis. Some trees have fallen nearby, from the immense weight of the snow and ice from freezing rain. They split and make a loud sound not heard in many years. No tipis are hit, but the noise does wake many villagers often during the long nights of the storm's fury cast upon the land of the Oglala Lakota.

Wanagiyata has been thinking, while snow bound, about going to the Pawnee village of Chief Bear (kuúruks – Pawnee dialect) Claw (aspiitu' – Pawnee dialect) and inviting him to bring his villagers to the spring powwow. He will ask his father, Chief Matoskah, for his permission to go after the white out passes from the village. He is not alone in wishing this restriction of movement to end and feeling a prisoner of one's tipi. The white out is so severe, with blowing thick snowflakes, that you could lose sight of your tipi if you tried to go more than fifty feet away and end up freezing to death. It is good that many days wood supply has been stored in all the village tipis. Being prepared for hardship is part of Chief Matoskah leadership abilities.

After the white out has passed, and the Oglala Lakota villagers come out of their tipis they see there is snow chest high on a šunkawakan (a horse), covering everything. Many trees near the village are stripped of their limbs and some blown over. Once the snow melts, gathering a new wood supply will be easier than ever to resupply. Nature has given the weak trees a haircut. The sun has broken through at last and the heavy snow covering begins to melt. It will be muddy for a while, but soon all will be back to normal winter days.

Permission has been given for Wanagiyata to go to the Pawnee village and invite Chief Bear Claw and his villagers to join the Chippewa and Crow at the Oglala Lakota village for powwow, set for early spring. He will leave as soon as the snow load has cleared and take his familiar team of Luzahan, Ciqala and his šungmanitu scout, Šungmanitu Ruler on this mission.

The three Oglala Lakota braves and Šungmanitu Ruler have pushed through some areas of heavy snow with their strong

šunkawakans. They are one days travel out from the Pawnee village and are going to make camp for the night soon, near a mountain stream running with fast waters from the snow melt of the white out. They reach the mountain stream

81

with about an hour's light left to make camp. Ciqala tends the horses, setting out a tie line and he hobbles (tie or strap together legs of a horse, or other animal to prevent it from straying) them with leather straps after they have had water to drink from the stream.

Three of the spare horses have been loaded with dried grass gathered and stored for winter feeding along with some corn, which is easier to travel with and pack on the horses. This supply of feed is welcomed by the horses, as they whinny when they know Ciqala is going to feed them.

Luzahan has gathered some wood to feed a fire all night and Wanagiyata has started a small fire and then gathered some pine needles for the three to bed down on with three tatanka hides stretched over some low hanging limbs for cover and they will sleep in their buffalo robes on top of the pine needles off the cold ground.

 The three Oglala Lakota braves, best of friends, work good together as a team, and soon enjoy a large warm fire near their tethered (tie an animal with rope or chain so as to restrict its movement) šunkawakans and eat some sintehanska (whitetail deer) Luzahan brought down with his bow not more than an hour ago. This hot food is a blessing, as the cold makes for a hard day's travel and this is a great end of the day time to share some stories around the campfire. Šungmanitu Ruler has eaten his fill and lies close to the fire one the edge of the pine needle bed made for sleeping human friends and will keep one eye open to guard during the night.

Wanagiyata keeps the fire going all night so they can sleep

with its warm glow crackling and popping with its very own language. Ciqala is first up and puts more wood on the fire and feeds the šunkawakans as daylight glides slowly in exposing their camp. After a good hot meal of more sintehanska meat, they pack up the remaining frozen deer meat, to take to Chief Bear Claw if he would like to have it, or they will use it on the return trip to their village and Šungmanitu Ruler will surely finish it.

Late in the day the Oglala Lakota braves reach the outskirts of the Pawnee village and are confronted by the guard set out about two hundred yards from the main village. They show their hands empty of any weapons and the alarm is sounded and many braves surround them and move them into meet with their great Chief Bear Claw.

The Pawnee braves are not aggressive, as they recognize the Oglala Lakota and know they come in peace. Chief Bear Claw greets Wanagiyata, Luzahan, Ciqala and their wolf scout. The Pawnee marvel at the friendly wolf, as he walks by Wanagiyata's side and stops standing before Chief Bear Claw. "Welcome my Oglala Lakota friends, my heart carries joy to see you safely here. Come to my lodge and share my fire, we will eat and smoke the pipe," says Chief Bear Claw.

After a meal of hot stew, made with elk meat and chick peas and some unknown spice, which is a very tasty and welcomed hot dish after a cold day's travel before Wanagiyata plans to speak. Wanagiyata speaks up, "Thank you Chief Bear Claw, for your welcome, I have come to invite you and all Pawnee villagers to a powwow at our Oglala Lakota village in early spring when the trees bud with green. The powwow will be a gathering place for the Chippewa and Crow friends of the Oglala

83

Lakota. There will be a celebration with dancing and singing by each tribe and food will be the gift of friendship by my village.

"My father, Chief Matoskah, wishes also, your village to come with goods to trade, as there will be much trading among all tribes gathered. He requests of you, to send word to Chief Cougar Man of the Jicarilla Apache village to come as dakotas (friends or allies) to the powwow. What answer do I carry to my chief?"

Chief Bear Claw answers, "It will be a great time to be alive and smoke the pipe among friends and to trade is good, I will not miss a 'good trade,' even with a Jicarilla Apache, as my trading skill is like the fox. I will send a scout to Chief Cougar Man with Chief Matoskah's invitation.

"Wanagiyata, I am pleased by your coming; we have some who suffer among our village. One child of seven winters, suffers a game leg, he hops and cannot walk. Another, a maiden was attacked by a kuúruks (bear – Pawnee dialect) waowešica (bear – Lakota dialect) and mauled, she is near death. A Pawnee boy is down with bad break high in his leg, he fell from cliff with snow many moons ago.

"Medicine man cannot heal; I think he needs power like you. Would you call to your God, to heal them as you did for me and  healing all my wounded braves who came against you"? "Take me to them now, as they should not suffer while I sit in comfort by your fire," responds Wanagiyata. "Follow, we go," says Chief Bear Claw with a big smile across his face. He thinks to himself that Wanagiyata is truly one whose heart comes from the land of spirits and he is truly a good human being.

Chief Bear Claw goes to the first lodge and tells the mother and father that he has brought a great healer to tend to their daughter. The four enter and go to the injured girl. Wanagiyata kneels by her side and sees her head and face have been ripped with bite marks and her scalp torn, she has a broken arm with bite marks and her buttocks has been bitten and torn, her right leg is torn deeply at the calf. It is a miracle that she has lived for two months, her mother has tended her faithfully, but she is now unconscious and dying.

Wanagiyata asks all to leave the lodge, as he needs to pray for this injured Pawnee maiden alone. Everyone leaves, and Wanagiyata begins his prayer. "My Wakantanka, my Father above, please let Your love pass through me to heal those in need, while I am here among the Pawnee. Let them know Your power and mercy and many may believe." Wanagiyata places his hand on the young maiden's head and soon her head and face are restored to their original beauty and her other wounds are healed along with her broken arm. Wakantanka has given Wanagiyata his healing powers.

The maiden wakes up and is unafraid, and thinks she may be in Mahpiya (Heaven, the clouds, the afterlife of mankind). She slowly wakes up, taken back to reality. Wanagiyata holds out his hand as he looks into her eyes. She takes his hand, and reality sets in, and she smiles as she stands and he leads her out of the family lodge by Wanagiyata. All who see her well and whole, fall to their knees and hold their arms up reaching toward the sky.

Her mother and father rush to her and hug her and then they thank Wanagiyata touching his arms and nodding their heads and her father says, "You will always be my friend forever into the unknown." "All thanks to be given to Wakantanka, I am only His servant," says Wanagiyata in the Pawnee dialect and this is also, astounding to all who hear his words in their own dialect.

"Chief Bear Claw, take me to all who need healing," states Wanagiyata. The healing of the boy who fell off a cliff was met with great joy to both parents and the young boy, who could not walk and now can run, cries tears of joy. The boy born with one leg shorter than the other, and had to hop on his one good leg was healed and he also walked out of his wakihiyece's lodge and into their arms. There was great joy among all in the village and even though it was cold, there was a great celebration to honor the 'Healer' and his companions including Šungmanitu Ruler, a real star among the children, as he let them pet him, without complaint, he is glad for the attention from his little Pawnee friends.

As everyone was having a great time, Wanagiyata was being served some food by an old Pawnee women, she looked at him and smiled a toothless smile and Wanagiyata took her empty hand in his, stood up and touched her closed mouth with the palm of his hand and looked upward and when he withdrew his hand the old women opened her mouth and all her teeth had been restored to the likeness of her youth. She thanked him and then started running among the Pawnee villagers and smiling her new smile, white young teeth shinning at each and every one. The celebration became even louder with joy and amazement at the wonders of this Oglala Lakota healer's kind deeds toward their tribe.

Chief Bear Claw called a halt to the dancing, singing and chanting and all went silent. He declared that the village would go to powwow with the Oglala Lakota, Chippewa, Crow and maybe even the Jicarilla Apache —if that would be their wish— in early spring time and that trading would be done along with much celebration. This news was taken with great joy and the celebration went late into the night. Chief Bear Claw invited his guest to stay in his large lodge and even Šungmanitu Ruler was welcomed in. He came in and was fed and then he went by the lodge entrance and fell asleep. It was not long before all were fast asleep in the warm Pawnee wigwam covered with tatanka hides. Many stories would be told of the great day the Oglala Lakota 'Healer' came from Wakantanka to visit their village.

After a great early meal of buffalo meat stew and some dried fish, the three Oglala Lakota braves thanked both the Pawnee chief and his wife for their hospitality and rode off toward their village, as a light snow was silently falling around them and the silence with its glitter was magical. Hopefully the wind would not blow up facing them on their return to their village.

Until our next Campfire Story Telling – "Preparing for the Great Powwow," stay true to your faith in Wakantanka, for He is by your side always. Where you step, He steps, do not lead Him into the presence of evil.

Capa building a dam

Chapter 5

Preparing for the Great Powwow

It is mid-afternoon as Wanagiyata (in the land of spirits), Luzahan (swift) and Ciqala (little one) are heading back to their Oglala Lakota village, after visiting their new dakotas (allies or friends) the Pawnee in the village of Chief Bear Claw Pawnee Chief Bear (kuúruks – Pawnee dialect) Claw (aspiitu' – Pawnee dialect), to invite them to a powwow (a North American Indian gathering ceremony involving feasting, singing, dancing, and trading), that would be held near their Oglala Lakota village in early spring. There will be other tribes at the powwow to celebrate pride, a friendship celebration with dancing; by using

89

sign language making trading possible.

This will be the first powwow for the Oglala Lakota, Chippewa, Crow, Pawnee and Jicarilla Apache (see appendix page 214) tribes and each will  be showing off their culture with great pride and trading items of different tribal design. This will be a chance for many friendships to develop among the tribes who were, not so long-ago, enemies. All this is because of Tatanka Ska Son's coming to Earth and befriending our young Oglala Lakota braves, Wanagiyata, Luzahan and Ciqala, who have become great 'Story Tellers' bringing many stories of Wakantanka (God) and His Son, Tatanka Ska Son (white buffalo) Wanikiye (the Savior).

A steady snow has been falling with no wind and travel has been easy and peaceful with silence bringing the three braves to each hatch different thoughts in their minds. There is one likeness in their thoughts and that is about their brides to be and plans of how they will live and provide for new wives and still be able to carry out their missions, as may be directed by their Chief Matoskah (white bear) and Tatanka Ska Son. These thoughts are enjoyed, with some concern, but mostly they are excited at the thought of new adventure and learning.

Tatanka Ska Son has given the great gift of healing to Wanagiyata and he has used it well, healing many in his tribe and other tribes, which has made dakotas of them and brought many to believe in Wakantanka and His Son, Tatanka Ska Son. Luzahan and Ciqala have also been chosen to be 'Story Tellers' and help to pass the stories of Wakantanka's Wishes for His people to know and believe.

The journey home has been pleasant for winter weather, but that is changing rapidly. The wind is hallowing and the three young braves are looking for some shelter from what is becoming a furious blizzard with winds increasing drastically. The weather is turning into a life-threatening situation and the young braves have never seen a storm like this one before. The šunkawakans (horses) they are riding and the iwaglamnas (extra or fresh horses – Lakota dialect) are trying to protect themselves by stopping and turning, facing away from the blowing snow and heavy winds. The three young braves pull all the horses together in a group and stand in the middle of them for some protection. Wanagiyata knows they are in deep trouble and calls on Tatanka Ska Son in prayer for help.

Soon after his prayer, Tatanka Ska Son appears to them in the blowing snow and tells them to follow him. Each brave leads two horses tethered (tie an animal with rope or chain so as to restrict its movement) together and they follow Him and soon they are led to a cave entrance. Inside the cave entrance is a campfire visible as they enter out of the raging storm. The cave has plenty of room for the braves and their šunkawakans. Šungmanitu (a wolf) Aitancan (the ruler over) is last to enter and shakes himself off, ridding his gray furry coat of cold snow. Tatanka Ska Son leads the Oglala Lakota braves to a large campfire with a pile of wood cut and stacked nearby. The three braves go to their knees in respect to Tatanka Ska Son. "Thank you, our dear Wanikiye (the Savior);

You're truly a loving Master." "Your prayers will always be heard if you believe in Me and My Father, Wakantanka, whenever you pray."

"Stand, feed and water your horses, then cook some of your sintehanska (whitetail deer) meat. There is a small stream near your warm fire for all to drink. This storm will blow for two days, but you are safe. Rest for two days and begin your journey home. Luzahan and Ciqala you have been good servants, so to make you both better 'Story Tellers' I am gifting you both with the knowledge of all languages of any people you may encounter from this day forward. Also, Luzahan you will take the new name of Oyaka (to tell, report, relate – Lakota dialect), Ciqala will be known as Okolaya (to have as a friend – Lakota dialect).

"Wanagiyata tell your father, Matoskah, of My Wish that Luzahan and Ciqala are to have these new names, which they have earned," says Tatanka Ska Son. He wheels around and is gone headlong into the snow storm, as snow swirls around Him briefly, as He disappears.

Wanagiyata says, "What a blessing to be safe and warm and you Luzahan, with a new name of Oyaka and Ciqala you with the new name of Okolaya. These new names fit you both well. You both will be great 'Story Tellers' and help me spread the Words and Wishes of Wakantanka and His Son, Tatanka Ska Son (in Chippewa dialect)." Both Oyaka and Okolaya smile and Oyaka answers in Chippewa, "We have been blessed beyond the stars." Oyaka in Chippewa dialect, "My bride to be will be very happy that I can speak her tongue and speak to her parents and all her tribe."

Okolaya responds, "I will cook some hot venison while you two will water, feed and hobble (tie or strap together legs of a horse, or other animal to prevent it from straying) the horses, now that I am much taller today, my bride will be pleased, but she is still taller." "It is a 'good trade'," says Wanagiyata in Pawnee. All three laugh in understanding and thankfulness for being saved from the terrible storm raging blizzard outside their warm cave shelter provided by Tatanka Ska Son, along with new powers and new names. What Blessings they have received, along with their very lives.

The three braves spend two more days and then as the storm breaks off and passes over them, they once again head for their village. "We must remember this cave place, if it is needed again," says Okolaya. Oyaka nods his head in approval and Wanagiyata speaks up in Chippewa dialect, "You are wise and you seem taller to me." All three braves laugh as they prod their šunkawakans through the deep snow as they make their way back to families and friends in the snow-covered Oglala Lakota village.

One day out from their tipis (teepee or lodge or tent), Okolaya spots a large sintesapela (the black tail or mule deer – Lakota dialect) and incredibly, he is able to speak in šungmanitu language, using various howling and sign language and has Wolf Ruler circle around and run the big buck back toward him and in range of his bow and arrow. The young Oglala Lakota braves will be even more welcomed bringing more food to the Oglala Lakota villagers.

Wanagiyata enters the village first and heads straight for Chief Matoskah's tipi. Chief Matoskah and Winona (first born daughter) greet their son with big smiles and invite the three young braves in to their tipi. Some of the braves take charge of the horses and tend to their needs, a gesture of respect for their brother warriors.

All three tell their stories to the chief and are fed by Winona and Wanagiyata's future wife, Wachiwi (dancing girl), even Šungmanitu Ruler is invited to lie near the entrance of the chief's tipi. He is welcome there; Chief Matoskah likes to see him there in comfort and throws him some food, which he catches in midair.

The chief's wife, Winona, and Wachiwi are very impressed by the great gifts of language and new names given by Tatanka Ska Son. Chief Matoskah has the three stay the night and rest and even Šungmanitu Ruler is welcomed and fed more.

The next day Chief Matoskah calls for celebration and tells the story of Tatanka Ska Son's gifts of many languages to Oyaka and Okolaya and assigning them their new names. The three young braves are highly revered among their tribal members. The day after the celebration of their return, Okolaya goes to the tipi of Kimimila (butterfly) and receives a warm welcome from her and his parents and spends the day with them in their warm tipi.

The snow is very deep and little hunting has been possible. The mule deer they brought in was gone the night of the celebration for their safe return. The blood brothers decide to go out with their horses and look for a moose or any deer they can find. The tatanka herds are far away and not accessible, until travel is easier and long-distance hunting is possible. They will take Šungmanitu Ruler with them; he can find game animals better than any man or animal. He has gone back to his wolf pack to check on them and will be back after he hunts down an elk for them. He returns the next day and Wanagiyata, Oyaka, Okolaya and Šungmanitu Ruler leave the village and begin the moose hunt.

Šungmanitu Ruler takes the lead and swings back and forth across the trail the braves are riding on. They are leading iwaglamnas, to carry any game they can kill, hopefully a tanka

(large, great in any way – Lakota dialect) takiyuha (bull – Lakota dialect) moose. Two miles out from the Oglala Lakota village ever faithful Šungmanitu Ruler, picks up the trail of a big bull moose and the hunters start following his trail in the deep snow.

Soon they spot him nibbling on some small tree branches. The three hunters split off and try to surround the huge moose, with their wolf friend holding in place, until needed if the moose gets past the young braves. The moose can run faster in the deep snow than they can on their horses, but he can't out run Šungmanitu Ruler, whose big padded paws keep him mostly on top of deep snow.

Okolaya closes in on the big moose and then when he is about one hundred feet away, he dismounts, ties his horse to a tree limb and starts to close in on the big moose with his spear. The moose hears Wanagiyata as he moves in on his horse. He turns and begins to run in Okolaya's direction, charging straight at him. He is about twenty-five feet away, when Okolaya throws his spear with all his might.

His spear hits the heyuȟa (the name of all animals with branching horns – Lakota dialect) high on the right shoulder and goes in deep, but it does not stop his charge. Just as the moose is

about to gore Okolaya with his huge rack of antlers seemingly, out of nowhere Šungmanitu Ruler has launched himself at the huge moose and he turns the charge away from Okolaya. The charging bull moose, catches Šungmanitu Ruler with his huge rack of antlers and throws him up and over his huge head and keeps running.

Wanagiyata closes in on the fleeing moose and puts two arrows in him and he goes down in the deep snow and Wanagiyata quickly dismounts and approaches the moose slowly to see if there is any life left in the huge moose. He waits until he is sure he is dead and then prods him with his bow to see if he is truly dead. He is and so Wanagiyata cuts into his belly and begins to field dress the huge animal. He is unaware of what has happened to Šungmanitu Ruler.

Okolaya goes to see how badly hurt his šungmanitu hero is. Šungmanitu Ruler has surely saved his life this day. He is bleeding badly; he has been gored in the side by the sharp horns on the end of the big moose's huge rack of antlers. He also, has some broken ribs and cannot get up. He is lying quietly breathing short breaths, because of his broken ribs and is in terrible pain.

Okolaya calls out for Wanagiyata and Oyaka to come quickly to help save their dear šungmanitu friend. Wanagiyata stops 'field dressing' the big moose and gets on his horse and heads over to Šungmanitu Ruler's side. Oyaka is already there and asked, "Can you heal him brother? He is in a lot of pain and can hardly take the air of life."

Wanagiyata raises his hands up and prays for his healing powers, soon he feels the warmth of his healing powers run through him and he places his hands on Šungmanitu Ruler's side

where he is wounded and watches his eyes as they brighten up and his tail starts to wag swiping the snow, like a tall spruce tree in a wind driven snow storm. Šungmanitu Ruler jumps up and starts to nuzzle

his healer. He is whole again and is running around in circles and stops to howl in a loud voice, joy has filled his heart once again and fresh air fills his lungs with new strength.

Okolaya tells his brother braves, how Šungmanitu Ruler saved his life and the brothers are all very happy and praise the šungmanitu brother and give him the moose heart to eat when they field dress the great moose. They load the moose meat on the spare horses and head for their village, with a great story to tell and precious moose meat for the Oglala Lakota villagers. Wakantanka is good to His young followers, He has blessed them with special gifts and brought them greatness and a high standing among their Oglala Lakota people, as will be true with other tribes they will encounter and help.

Šungmanitu Ruler is in the lead as he breaks the trail for his brother wahununpa (man in sacred language) Wanagiyata, who is riding behind him as he runs through the deep snow, followed by Oyaka and Okolaya with their spare horses loaded down with moose meat. They reach the village late in the afternoon, and all the villagers turn out from their tipis and Wanagiyata helps his brothers, give out meat to the women of each family. Chief Matoskah and wife are very pleased with the fresh meat. There will be a celebration this night and they will be told the story of the wolf, "Šungmanitu Aitancan's" heroism facing the charging big bull moose and saving Okolaya's life, with no concern for his own safety.

To risk one's own life to save a friend is the ultimate act of self-sacrifice one can give, a true test of the depth of a friendship. The greatest example of all was when Wanikiye gave His Human Life long ago to save us from our sins, that we would believe in Wakantanka and live with Him in Mahpiya (Heaven) forever. All this, because His Father, Wakantanka's Will was to sacrifice His only begotten Son to save all Mankind and give them everlasting life with Him.

Chief Matoskah is very impressed by Okolaya's story and when the entire village gathers to celebrate, he calls for silence and then speaks, "As you can see my son, Wanagiyata, has returned. The hunt was good, as you can see the moose meat our women are cok'in (to roast on spits over coals – Lakota dialect). Hunting the big bull moose nearly ended young Okolaya's life. The moose charged Okolaya and he threw his spear and wounded him, he was close to Okolaya and Šungmanitu Ruler took the charge to himself. He was broken and death was calling him, but Wanagiyata called on Wakantanka for the power of healing and Šungmanitu Ruler was made whole as you can

clearly see. From this day forward, any day he and his šungmanitu pack need our food or protection, it will be given freely. Before the killing of the sintesapela, by Wanagiyata, Okolaya, Oyaka, and Šungmanitu Ruler were caught in the same iyapa (a snow storm – Lakota dialect) that hit all tipis in our village. Tatanka Ska Son appeared and led them to a cave to shelter in. He saved all lives and šunkawakans and we must give thanks to Wakantanka for saving them once again from the takiyuha and providing this great takiyuha to feast on. Do so with no talk." All the villagers offer a silent prayer of thanks and then a great celebration begins.

Kimimila finds Okolaya and delivers some of the roasted moose meat from the one who almost killed him. Okolaya takes the moose meat to Šungmanitu Ruler and gives it to him to eat. Kimimila sees this act of honoring his šungmanitu friend and knows she has made the right choice for her future husband and goes to get another bowl of food for Okolaya. Oyaka, sees both his brothers being served with food by their future wives looking after them with great care and he is suddenly feeling very lonely, a true sign of being in love.

He can hardly wait for the early spring powwow. He takes

joy in his thoughts, thinking of the surprise all the Chippewa village and his father and mother in marriage will experience when he speaks their own tongue. He will surely be revered by them with his special powers of speech. His new gift of the knowledge of many languages sets him aside from all other Chippewa braves.

Most of all Oyaka is excited, that he will be able to gift Gidagaakoons (fawn – Chippewa dialect) with being able to speak her dialect at their wedding. He starts to smile as he will surprise her, her parents and all the Chippewa that attend the powwow. Then he has the thought, that his gift of speaking the Chippewa tongue will really help him in trading. He is starting to realize a small part of the greatness of his gift of many languages, for one, he can trade with all the tribes and help others with making a 'good trade'.

Wanagiyata, Oyaka, and Okolaya are all thinking about what they will be using for trading and they start to make weapons and pipes for smoking. They all have mares in foal and may trade the fouls if need be, but hopefully their trades will give them what they will need, to start their married life. They will need a minimum of, fourteen to sixteen tatanka (a male buffalo) hides for a good tipi and six more to lie on as beds off the cold ground and for entertaining guest to sit on.

The three Oglala Lakota braves have decided that they will go and hunt the tatanka. They will ask their fathers to go with them and others, who would be willing to give-up their buffalo hides to the three husbands to be as wedding gifts, but they will keep the meat for themselves.

Winter is breaking and Wanagiyata, Oyaka, and Okolaya, have been making good strong bows along with many straight quality arrows, some flint knives, some flint stone axes for chopping wood and some pipes for smoking. It is time to go hunt the tatanka herd and bring much needed food to the Oglala Lakota village, as the winter has been one of the worst in many years. The young brides to be, have been sewing tahakalalas (a buckskin dress – Lakota dialect), tahape wapoštan (a fur cap – Lakota dialect) and wanap'inkicaton (to put on as a piece of neckwear, to cause to wear as a necklace – Lakota dialect) to trade. Everyone has been busy making trade goods.

Gidagaakoons is in her Chippewa village and is a very good potter and has made many bowls and cups and some metates (see appendix page 216) of various shapes and sizes to grind grain. She also has made two mortars (a mortar is shaped like a bowl and made of stone) and pestles (a pestle is a blunt stone or stick used to pound seeds or grain into a mortar to crush them into meal). These can be heavy, so she will only take one to powwow, along with many bowls and cups. Her brother Ma'iingan (timber wolf – Chippewa dialect) will help her transport some of her trading goods, but most will be packed on travois (a type of sledge – Lakota dialect) pulled by her father's horses, along with his trade goods and he will walk along with the rest of the Chippewa villagers.

Chief Matoskah, Wanagiyata, Oyaka, Okolaya, Canška (red-legged hawk – Lakota dialect), Wanbligleška (the spotted eagle – Lakota dialect) and many Oglala Lakota braves, all with spare horses begin the hunt for buffalo. This hunt has a very important member, a great tracker and hunter in his own area of Mother Earth. Wanagiyata has called out to Šungmanitu Ruler and he will lead the hunt, along with two of his šungmanitu best trusted trackers from his pack.

If Wolf Ruler's pack has a problem finding game without his keen nose, they can go to the Oglala Lakota village and they will be fed and cared for. It is a 'good trade' of human to animal, animal to human symbiosis (interaction between two different organisms living in close physical association, typically to the advantage of both).

Two days out from their Oglala Lakota village, one of Šungmanitu Ruler's trackers has run across tatanka tracks and he lets out a long howl, alerting his wolf leader, that he has found the trail of a tatanka herd. Šungmanitu Ruler answers his tracker and then he speaks to Wanagiyata, who understands his signing completely. "My father, our faithful šungmanitu friends have found the trail of tatanka. Follow Šungmanitu Ruler, he will lead us now," says Wanagiyata. The hunting party speeds up their tracking of what appears to be a large herd of buffalo.

It is around three hours after sunrise, when the hunting party close in on the tatanka herd. They split off from each other and charge in from different directions on the panicked herd of buffalo, now in full flight. The sound is like thunder boiling from their cleft hooves as they pound the partially snow-covered turf. Chief Matoskah has spotted a big bull and closes in and launches his spear with great accuracy hitting the big bull tatanka in the heart. The big bull falls and slides to a halt in the snow. He continues his hunt and brings down another bull with two well-placed arrows. That is all the buffalo meat he can pack back to the village on his four iwaglamnas.

Almost all the hunting party have taken two buffalo each, some braves only killed one, but their horses will be used to haul the tatanka meat back to the village. It takes the rest of the day to field dress the tatankas taken in the hunt and load them and then find a good place to make camp for the night.

They find a small stream to pitch camp by and unload the tatanka meat, care for their horses, and then they all eat and put out guards for the night. They sleep soundly; it has been a long and hard day, but most rewarding thanks to their šungmanitu friends. The weather is very cold and that is good, because they can keep the meat fresh until they get back to their village and then the women will process the meat into jerky and then scrape the buffalo hides and make robes and blankets from them. Some will be saved for use to cover tipis.

Wanagiyata has the tipi from Wachiwi's parents who were killed by the renegade Chippewa Abooksigun (wildcat – Chippewa dialect). Okolaya has the tipi of Kimimila's parents who were also were killed by Abooksigun, so the only husband to be, who does not have his own tipi is Oyaka.

Wanagiyata and Okolaya, along with Chief Matoskah will give their tatanka hides to Oyaka, that makes six, plus he already has two from the hunt. He sleeps on one and covers with another in his parent's tipi. Now, Oyaka has a total of ten tatankas hides for his tipi. But soon Canška and Wanbligleška ride up to Oyaka on the return trip and tell him that they are giving him their tatanka hides as a wedding gift. He thanks them for their gifts. Now he has fourteen, he feels he can trade for more and have a lodge for his new bride. Life is so good when you have close friends who are kind and giving.

When the hunters enter the village many songs and chants welcome them. The women help with unloading the tatanka meat and the hides and start processing the meat and begin the smoking and making jerky. The hunters are tired and all eat and then get in their blankets as darkness rolls in on a joyous Oglala

Lakota village.

It is early morning when Wanagiyata is having his early meal and his name is called from outside his parent's tipi. He is needed for one of his brother braves wives is having trouble giving birth and is in great pain. When Wanagiyata enters the tipi of the birthing women, her husband and two Oglala Lakota women are trying to help her, but they can do no more. It is a breech birth (the baby is being born feet first instead of by the head).

Wanagiyata asks for hot water and begins to pray to Wakantanka for guidance. A silent Voice only heard by

Wanagiyata comes from Wakantanka and Wanagiyata places his hand on the bottom of the baby and pushes it back into the women and turns the baby around and brings the head into the correct birthing position. Soon with the help of strong pushing by the pregnant women's stomach muscles, a baby boy enters the world and begins to cry. The parents and the attending women, all cry out in happiness, and thank Wanagiyata for his healing hand. He tells them to thank Wakantanka and that he is only His messenger.

Until our next Campfire Story Telling – "The Great Oglala Lakota Powwow," may Wakantanka be your companion, talk to Him and He will answer.

Chapter 6

The Great Oglala Lakota Powwow

Chief Bagwungijik (hole in the sky – Chippewa dialect) has left his village with most of his Chippewa tribe heading for the Oglala Lakota powwow (a North American Indian gathering ceremony involving feasting, singing, dancing, and trading). He has his šunkawakans, —given to him by Chief Matoskah (white bear) of the Oglala Lakota as a gift of friendship, after they were at war two years ago— loaded down with trade goods. His wife, Amitola (rainbow – Chippewa dialect), and daughter, Gidagaakoons (fawn – Chippewa dialect), are more excited about the upcoming wedding where Gidagaakoons, will become the wife of the young highly respected Oglala Lakota brave, Oyaka (to tell, report, relate). This will be one of the rare weddings of persons of different tribes, cultures and languages. There will be a big surprise in store for all the Chippewa at the wedding to be held at the powwow. Along with all the ceremonial cultural performances of singing, dancing, chanting, and trading, there will be a surprise coming from Oyaka.

It is early spring; the green buds are popping out of the tree limbs, announcing spring and telling the story winter has passed. New life will show in many ways that Mother Earth is at work creating new life and caring for her children, who have been locked in the icy grip of winters' confines. All the creatures who live under ground or use her for cover, are appearing and many are hungry and that includes waoweŝicas (a bear in general) who have been living off the fat they have stored in the year past.

The capa (beaver – Lakota dialect) stayed in their lodges in the frozen waters of ponds they have created with their dam building skills, living off a cache of branches they stored under the ice stuck in the bottom of the pond for food to last through the hard winters. There are a few patches of snow in some shaded areas; however they are melting fast with spring presenting warmer winds to all she touches. The going is easy as the Chippewa village of Chief Bagwungijik travel toward the Oglala Lakota village.

The Crow tribe of Axxaashe (sun – Crow dialect) Bachhee (man – Crow dialect) formally known as Arikara (running wolf – Crow dialect), now known as 'Sun Man' to all others. A warrior blessed with great strength by Wakantanka (God) who is following behind his new Chief Chogan (blackbird – Algonquin dialect) leading his Crow villagers to meet with others that will attend the powwow.

His Oglala Lakota friends Wanagiyata (in the land of spirits), Oyaka and Okolaya (to have as a friend), who saved him from raiding Jicarilla Apache (see appendix page 214) braves, will be there to greet him. The great and most powerful Crow warrior is riding his very valuable šunkawakan (a horse) iichiile (horse – Crow dialect) given to him by Wanagiyata after he was saved and healed by the hand of Wanagiyata and his prayer to Wakantanka (God). Only Sun Man can ride him alone or care for his horse, as its welfare on which his great strength relies, has been directed by Wakantanka, as a show of faithfulness to Him. All the attending tribes have a common need that will come to light at powwow.

The Pawnee Chief Kuúruks Aspiitu' (bear claw – Pawnee dialect), Chief Bear Claw is leading his Pawnee villagers as spring has sprung to life. He has visited other Pawnee villages and told the campfire stories of Wanagiyata and the story of Sun Man the greatest warrior; he has ever battled against and lost in an overwhelming manner. He tells the story of the healing of all his wounded warriors and himself by Wanagiyata, who has the power of healing from Wakantanka.

Word of these two special warriors is spreading to other Pawnee villages; most do not believe it is possible, although some do. Chief Bear Claw will take gifts for Wanagiyata and his father, Chief Matoskah, who is hosting the powwow as a good will gesture. His medicine man is hoping he can gain the healing powers that Wanagiyata has, but that will not happen, his heart is not good, for he only seeks power among his Pawnee villagers to have more control over them to benefit himself.

Apache Chief Ndolkan (cougar – Apache dialect) Homme (man – Apache dialect) is leading many Jicarilla Apache from his village to the powwow and they are loaded down with goods to trade. Their šunkas (dogs - Lakota dialect) have travois (a type of sledge) attached to them loaded with buffalo hides for their tipis (teepee or tent or lodge) to be used when they setup their camp at powwow. Some dogs are pulling trade goods and cooking pots. The women are loaded down, some with small children, some with a cinca (a child) bound up and strapped to a board which is carried by its mother. It looks like a migration, for all the visiting tribes will need their own tipis, blankets, cooking items, dried legumes (a seed, pod, or other edible part of leguminous plant, used for food), and smoked meat. Hopefully, they can hunt and fish for fresh food along the way.

Everyone, who will attend the powwow, is excited thinking about being able to meet all the different tribal members and to be able to show their dress costumes, showing their cultural heritage and tribal customs through song and dance. This will be the first time the different tribes will be trading with tribes that were in the past enemies until recently. All because of mercy and forgiveness shown by Wanagiyata and his father Chief Matoskah, taught by Tatanka Ska Son.

Back at the Oglala Lakota village, an area one mile away has been selected by Chief Matoskah near water and a large grass covered open space, where all the visiting tribes can make camp

108

and have the water nearby. Many of the Oglala Lakota women and boys have been gathering wood and storing it nearby for the powwow tribes attending, to use. Also, many braves have been hunting tatanka and the women have been making jerky and smoking meat from hehaka (the male elk) and a rare moose hunted by the braves, before they left on a big buffalo hunt. The village is buzzing like a bee hive with everyone making trading goods and preparing their best tribal attire.

Three future brides have been very busy making gifts for their future husbands for months. The weddings for Wachiwi (dancing girl) and Kimimila (butterfly) are very soon. They have become best friends and have had each other to share in helping make their wedding costumes. The help of Winona (first born daughter), mother of Wanagiyata and wife of Chief Matoskah has also helped design the costumes. Winona has taken in Wachiwi as a daughter, since her parents and Kimimila's parents were killed by the raiding Chippewa named Abooksigun (wildcat – Chippewa dialect).

Oglala Lakota weddings were simple, the brave brought gifts to the father of the bride and if he thought the brave was good and excepted his gifts, the brave would take his wife he had purchased and that was the custom. It would change many years later, when the white man would come. However, a good father would consider his daughter's choice, if he could approve of her choice in husbands. Brides were bought and that was the custom of the Oglala Lakota Indians. The couples were considered living in marriage by the villagers, they were only held together by caring for one another. If they did not want to be together, they simply gathered their personal things and went their own way. Those who stayed together were those who treated each other with respect, having children most often keep the parents close together as a family unit. That practice was the custom of the Oglala Lakota.

Chief Bagwungijik's daughter, Gidagaakoons, has chosen to sing a song as she is handed over to Oyaka, the future bride or groom must have gifts for all immediate guests, in keeping with what they can make or buy or trade for. She has many small gifts and has been helped by many of her villagers. Who respect her choice in husbands and his friendship with the 'Great Healer', Wanagiyata, and most want to attend.

The giving of gifts to all who attend the 'Give Away', is considered the Chippewa way of taking a wife in their custom. Oyaka, has already given the price Chief Bagwungijik has asked for his payment for Gidagaakoons, but he chose to wait until the powwow to have the 'Give Away' to conclude the marriage and include his parents and friends. The bride's song is beautiful and she will try to use sign language along with her Chippewa words to tell the story, so Oyaka's parents and other Oglala Lakota may understand some of her song to him.

Chief Bagwungijik's tribe is one day out from reaching the Oglala Lakota village and scouts have told Chief Matoskah of their location. He will take his son and Oyaka and ride out to greet them and show them were to setup camp. The three Oglala Lakota friends have decided to have their purchases and 'Give Away' to happen at the same time, as they will always be friends, as like unto blood related brothers. Their friendship will be for life, as it has been in their youth.

When the greeting party meet up with the Chippewa villagers, Chief Matoskah has brought a spare horse for Chief Bagwungijik and his wife, Amitola, to ride, and Oyaka pulls his future bride, Gidagaakoons, up behind him on his šunkawakan (a horse). Then he has her brother, his friend, Ma'iingan (timber wolf – Chippewa dialect), mount his iwaglamna (an extra or fresh horse) and he leads him as they walk the horses to the campground site of the powwow. Chief Matoskah has brought some other Oglala Lakota braves to help the Chippewa set up camp.

The Chippewa are first to arrive and setup very close to a stream fed by mountain snows, the sound it makes is Mother Earth's song especially at night when the winds are still. The Chippewa guests are provided with fresh meat and some dried beans and corn, along with some elk jerky and smoked moose meat. They will all share in fresh tatanka meat when powwow starts.

The Crow villagers led by their Crow Chief Chogan and the powerful Sun Man are next to come in and are escorted to the camp ground. By Wanagiyata and they are afforded the same warm welcome the Chippewa received. The Crow are helped setting up their camp and also, receive food and begin to settle in, making camp.

Pawnee Chief Bear Claw arrives the next day and is greeted by Wanagiyata and is led to the powwow location and set up his camp near the Crow villagers alongside the great and powerful Sun Man, who is now friendly to him. They greet each other and their words are translated by Wanagiyata. Chief Bear Claw invites Sun Man and Wanagiyata into his tipi to smoke a pipe and it is a good feeling by a warm fire, with new friends.

The Jicarilla Apache arrive two days later with Chief Cougar Man. He towers over all others who are in attendance at the powwow. He is very kind and mannerly, after being defeated and had his life spared by Sun Man of the Crow Nation.

All the chiefs gather in Chief Bear Claw's Pawnee tipi along with Wanagiyata, Oyaka, Ma'iingan, Okolaya, and Crow Chief Chogan with Sun Man are invited to attend the night of the Jicarilla Apache's arrival to smoke the pipe. The official start for the powwow will begin in the morning, when all the Oglala Lakota villagers arrive and occupy their temporary camp filled with trading goods and ceremonial dress and drums, etc.

It is a busy night as most are getting ready for trading. The powwow will start around early afternoon, but first there will be a most wonderful beginning that could seal the friendship of all attending this powwow. The chiefs while smoking have asked Wanagiyata if he will honor them with his special gift of healing, because each chief has brought all the sick and infirmed of their tribe with them in the hope that he will heal them all. Wanagiyata told them, it would be his joy to have them all gather in one area in front of all the Indian Nations at the powwow and he would do his best to call on Wakantanka for his healing powers.

All the tribes at powwow have brought their sick and infirmed and placed them before an area chosen by Wanagiyata for his attempt to make them whole. The entire gathering has gone quiet as Wanagiyata calls on his God, Wakantanka, for the healing power he requires to help all those in need. He does not feel the healing powers flow though him and is praying again. The sky goes darker and then a shaft of light appears across the sky and all see this great light and are scared to the last brave, watching in wonder.

The shaft of light brightens and as it travels toward the direction of the powwow and it forms a tunnel of bright colors, as it lands in front of Wanagiyata and all those gathered in anticipation of a miracle of healing which some were beginning to have doubts of his powers. From the mouth of the multi-colored tube appears Tatanka Ska Son (Son of Wakantanka) in all His Glory, His white fur gleaming and His blue eyes speaking a message of love and kindness. All present, dropped to their knees in a humble show of respect.

Tatanka Ska Son begins to speak in a Voice heard by all and in the language each one speaks and understands, "Fear not, for I come to show you I am real, and My 'Story Tellers', Wanagiyata, Oyaka, and Okolaya are to be revered among all, for they carry My Words, which come from My Father, Wakantanka. Wanagiyata was about to heal these gathered before Me, however, some doubted his gift from My Father, Wakantanka. In order that you should believe in Me, I have come to heal all those who need My Father's help. Father, I call on You to heal all here before Me, that others may see Your Power and Love for them."

Silence is complete, even the water running fast in the mountain stream nearby has stopped and all of nature has gone quiet. A long minute passes and Tatanka Ska Son turns and enters the tunnel of multi-colored light, which brightens as He enters. It then moves silently away across the sky and disappears behind the moon, which is alight in soft blue color and clearly seen in the dimmed daylight.

The silence is broken by a scream of joy —heard by all in their own dialect— "I can see! I can see!" shouts a Jicarilla Apache woman, totally blind from birth, shattering the total

113

silence. A young Pawnee boy is on his feet and cries out, "I can stand and I can walk." A Chippewa baby held by her mother cries in her mother's arms, it is the first sound ever from this baby girl. The mother stands and shows the baby to everyone and says, "My baby has sound, she will make the talk." All those who were sick and afflicted by any abnormality, speak out in great joy. Sounds of parents and friends and other family members present, fills the air.

As astounding as the visit and healing by Tatanka Ska Son has been, the aftermath of the amazing miracles continues to be revived consisting of the mountain stream stopping and all nature going silent. Also, amazing is the fact that every word of all those healed are understood by all in their own dialect, is realized long after Tatanka Ska Son has departed.

Soon all of Mother Earth's creatures are heard singing out in their own song. The šungmanitu (a wolf) pack nearby howl, the šunkmanitus (coyotes) group yip-howls are heard further away, birds unite in song. Crickets buzz and zicaȟota (gray squirrel – Lakota dialect) scamper around as a waš'in (bull frog – Lakota dialect) makes a deep snorting sound almost like a wild kukuše (pig – Lakota dialect). Even the sound of a capa (beaver) slapping his big flat tail can be heard, all these sounds, a song sung in unison orchestrated by Mother Earth's hand, as she honors Wakantanka and His Son, Tatanka Ska Son.

All the different tribes gather near to those who have been healed and great joy is shared by all for a short time, then Oglala Lakota Chief Matoskah calls for silence and he speaks, "Welcome, dakotas (allies or friends) to our first powwow. My son, Wanagiyata, will speak in all tongues spoken here among your tribes. All thanks to Wakantanka and His Son, Tatanka Ska

Son, for His healing and blessings. You, present this day, have seen and with eyes and heard with ears, the Words of the Son of Wakantanka and seen His Power. Let this story be heard by all at many campfires by those who have knowledge.

"The trading will begin, then the taking of three brides shall pass on to husbands and for those invited to see. Next, a meal, a gift from the Oglala Lakota village to our new dakotas. The Jicarilla Apache will dance the dance and sing the song tonight until we must go to our blankets with joy and okit'a (to be tired, fatigued – Lakota dialect)." Wanagiyata speaks in all languages the words spoken by his father, Chief Matoskah. This is further proof of the abilities of this messenger from Wakantanka and His Son, Tatanka Ska Son.

The next day women of the entire Oglala Lakota village cook and serve all the guest oyate (a people, nation, tribe or band) with their very best food fare, tatanka, heȟaka, hogleglega (the grass pike or perhaps also the rainbow fish) and sintesapela (the black-tail deer or mule deer). Bean and corn soups and stews are also, served with pride. It is a feast all will remember.

It is time for the simple traditional weddings to take place. The future brides and their braves, along with family, friends and invited guest are gathered beside a quieter section of the beautiful mountain stream. Chief Matoskah, with tawicu (his wife), Winona, beside him, steps forward and takes the hand of Wachiwi and Wanagiyata and gives each the hand of the other. Then places his hand on their heads and says, "It is well." They are now considered married.

A great whopping sound erupts from the families and all guests. It is time for Okolaya and Kimimila, to have the same simple ceremony and blessing by Okolaya's father, Šungila (fox

– Lakota dialect) father of Okolaya and guardian of Kimimila, since her parents were killed by Abooksigun, the Chippewa raider.

Šungila and his wife face Okolaya and Kimimila and Šungila speaks up, "Okolaya, take the hand of Kimimila, you have brought me what I requested for her hand, now she is yours. Her mother and I bless this union." Okolaya and Kimimila look deep into the eyes of one another and step beside Wanagiyata and Wachiwi, as both couples wait to see the marriage of Oyaka and Gidagaakoons, his Chippewa future bride.

Chief Bagwungijik and his wife Amitola, stand in front of their daughter, Gidagaakoons, and Oyaka, and the chief says "Oyaka, you have given what I required of you some moons ago, now you and my daughter, Gidagaakoons, pass on your gifts to your brother Ma'iingan and your invited ones then come back to stand before me."

The young couple pass out many small presents to their invited ones, and then Oyaka walks to Canška (red-legged hawk) and takes the lead-line hooked to a šunkawakan tawanap'in (a horse collar – Lakota dialect) of a šunkawakan and leads him to Ma'iingan and hands the lead-line to him. Ma'iingan breaks into a big smile and thanks his new brother-in-marriage-to-be. This is a most special gift and a bond representing true brotherhood between the young braves of different tribes, until they must 'walk on'.

Oyaka and Gidagaakoons return and face her parents and Gidagaakoons takes Oyaka's hand and says in her Chippewa dialect, "I could not walk beside the whispering clear waters of a mountain stream and not think of you who calm my fears." She points toward the mountain stream and moves her free hand in sign language. "I could not see the mountain high without seeing you taller in my mind." She signs pointing to the mountains and then puts her free hand high above his head in sign language. "I could not hold another in my heart, which you carry away where travels take you and I am alone." She now holds her hand over her heart in sign. "My heart is filled with joy and my mind runs before me, as we become one people. I wish you could understand my words, as I have spoken. Wanagiyata please speak my words to my husband."

Oyaka is truly moved by the words of Gidagaakoons and she is puzzled by the emotion she sees in his eyes. Oyaka speaks softly "It is I, who am alone as you are not by my side." Oyaka sees the shock of all who hear him speak in Chippewa dialect and continues speaking. "This, my bride, is my gift to you, your family and all Chippewa villagers I now belong to in a family way. This gift was given to me by Wakantanka.

"I will be a 'Story Teller' for all the Chippewa Nation, as you and I grow in love and walk hand in hand to the end of the river of life." Gidagaakoons rushes into Oyaka's arms and the two hold each other with great joy. Chief Bagwungijik speaks, "The marriage is blessed and I will smoke the pipe and see the Jicarilla Apache dancing with a happy heart, for it is so."

The three newlywed couples and great friends, all gather near to watch the show the Jicarilla Apache are about to perform. The entire tribes now dakotas, gathered at powwow are seated on blankets in a huge circle, as Chief Cougar Man leads his warriors into the center of the circle. The great chief is striking in his deerskin pants and shirt, with many colored beads sewn into the sleeves and arranged in designs of mountain lions on each side of his tan shirt. His head dress is enormous and the eagle feathers stick upward, from his headdress and make him look to be over eight foot tall.

He presents a formidable presence and all who see him are glad he is a dakota, save one, Sun Man, who is the greatest warrior to ever live. He is now watching Chief Cougar Man closely to see if his spirit is good. It is good that they are together here and with the help of one of the three 'Chosen Ones', Wanagiyata, Oyaka, and Okolaya, to help interpret for them, they will become fast friends before the powwow ends.

The dancing, chanting and songs of the Jicarilla Apache villagers is most impressive and very few leave before the

ceremonial performance is over late into the night. The day has been one of wonder and great joy, with the appearance of Tatanka Ska Son and the miraculous healing of all those who have come to be made whole. Truly, many now believe in Wakantanka and His Son, Tatanka Ska Son.

Tomorrow's light will be the start of day trading, then a meal will be served to all attending the powwow, and trading will continue until evening food has been eaten by each tribe in their own camp. All tribes gather at sunset for the Chippewa to perform and show their cultural trappings (the outward signs, features). In the meantime, our married couples have gone off to themselves, where love will be shared, as is the custom of young love in a new marriage to be consummated.

Chief Bagwungijik, followed by his son, Ma'iingan, leads the rest of the Chippewa dancers in the circle and begin the dancing and singing of songs. They are highly trained and they show that they perform in a more controlled and subdued manner than the Jicarilla Apache, however they do perform a war dance, which is fearsome in its dance moves to the drum beat. All enjoy and cheer, even the Jicarilla Apache are impressed and pleased by the Chippewa performance.

The next day consists of day long trading and then a feast, once again provided by the Oglala Lakota villagers. It is then followed by the ceremonial performance of the Crow village of Sun Man. The Crow dancers and drummers enter the circle by the large campfire and begin to dance, chant and sing. Many songs are performed, but Sun Man is nowhere to be found and all attending are puzzled why it was not him leading his people into entertain at the powwow.

Soon, the sound of a screaming chant is heard outside the circle and it grows louder in the darkness as the screaming chant draws nearer the circle by the campfire. It is Sun Man, mostly carrying two tatankas held off the ground. He ran out of camp earlier in the day hunted down and killed them, some ten miles away and is carrying each one by a horn in his most powerful hands.

As he enters all his dancers and drummers move out of his

way, as he runs around the campfire with the two huge tatanka in tow. He is running at a tremendous speed, throwing some grass in the air from the rear of the tatanka's rumps and their cloven hooves which are tearing at the turf as they are being dragged around by Sun Man.

The entire Indian Nations in attendance are completely awed by this unbelievable site of inhuman strength taking place before their very eyes. Sun Man stops before Chief Matoskah and delivers the two tatankas to him as a gift, his thoughtful way of helping to share the burden of all the Oglala Lakota who have been providing most of the food, which they have so freely given to all at powwow. All the tribes are now standing in astonishment and some in a fearful manner.

Chief Matoskah thanks Sun Man and invites him to sit beside him. Sun Man instructs his Crow dancers and drummers to continue their performance. When the ceremony is complete Sun Man takes the tatanka to where the Oglala Lakota women want them placed and hangs them up to be dressed out for cooking or smoking as they please. The total Crow performance, including that of Sun Man, will be very hard to top.

The next day trading again finds many trying to trade, but having some trouble communicating, so now the three brother braves with powers of all dialects are called on to help in the haggling and are most popular among the traders with their super natural skills. It is great fun and many are laughing as various trades take place, some make bad trades, but seem happy, all of which is in the mind of the beholder. Personally Wanagiyata, Oyaka and Okolaya, make very good trades for items their new wives need, being directed to those treasures by each new bride. Such is the way, when building a new life in one's own tipi to face the cold and rain in comfort together; a good wife is a treasure to men, like no other.

More trading is the fare of the day and then, as evening approaches, more food is greatly enjoyed in each separate tribal camp, before all gather to see the Pawnee villagers ceremony performed later that night. Chief Bear Claw leads his warriors and some female dancers in to the entertainment campfire circle and they begin to dance to the rapid beat of the Pawnee drummers. The ceremony is very lively and all the dancers have left all they have to give in their performance by the fire. They are all blokit'a (to be very tired, weary, exhausted – Lakota dialect).

The next and final day of the powwow, a great tragedy has occurred. During the night one Chief Bear Claw's daughters dies of a heart attack, and is found cold in her blanket, by her mother, and all are sad at her passing. The Pawnee trading will be limited; however the Pawnee will attend the final night's festivities after a feast once again provided by the Oglala Lakota villager's great generosity.

Chief Matoskah and his family, are very troubled by the loss of Chief Bear Claw's young daughter, but must try to provide a great celebration and performance for their new dakotas and try to be respected with their talents in entertaining and showing their cultural heritage. After the final feast of fresh tatanka, furnished by Sun Man, and many bean and grain dishes, along with dried berries are also served. Chief Matoskah stands and all goes silent in respect for his words to be spoken. Chief Matoskah speaks up, "My dakotas, my son, Wanagiyata, will speak for me and that is all I have to say."

Wanagiyata stands and steps beside his father, who steps one pace backward. In words of all the tribes gathered here, he speaks, "We have come to know each other as dakotas and many trades have been made. Most of all trades were good and you have seen and heard Tatanka Ska Son and seen His Healing Powers, for all who needed them. Now I will call upon Chief Bear Claw to bring his daughter before me, that I may pray to Wakantanka for her spirit." Chief Bear Claw rushes to his tipi and he and his wife carry their daughter wrapped in a blanket and place her softly down before Wanagiyata and each, take one step backward.

All is in total silence and as Wanagiyata begins to pray, the mountain stream once again comes to a standstill, along with all animals in the woods. No sound from any creature of the night is heard, all is completely silent. Wanagiyata has been praying in silence with his hand lifted high reaching up to Wakantanka for his healing powers, then his voice is heard in all dialects, "My God, Wakantanka, I call on You to restore the spirit of Chief Bear Claw and Amatole's daughter to them, for she is young and has not had Your works and her kindhearted gifts to give to all in this life, as You might like her to have given to Your children, all in Your Precious Name. If it is Your Will, please, I ask in the Name of Your Son, Tatanka Ska Son, to restore her spirit to those who love her. This is my prayer, oh Great One," prays Wanagiyata.

Great thunder erupts and many lightning flashes cross the sky and light all around those standing in fear, but trusting, that no harm will come to them. Because they believe that Wanagiyata is standing with them. They have seen Tatanka Ska Son and some of His miracles and power and they believe they are safe. More flashes of lighting without the thunder are going in all directions across the night's sky, maintaining a constant bright light by the rapid succession of striking lightning bolts.

Soon in the flashing silence, movement begins in the blanket and is seen by Chief Bear Claw and his tawicu, Amitola. Soon there is a strong struggle going on in the blanket. Chief Bear Claw kneels and frees his daughter from her blanket, she is wide

eyed as a young deer and all the silence is broken by screams of joy that builds, as all who cannot see what has happened, begin to understand. That the young one who was lost to them and dead to this world, has returned to

live again among them. It is a greatest of miracles and all go to a kneeling position and raise their hands and eyes up to Wakantanka in praise and thanks.

Chief Matoskah watches in wonder the power given to his son and he is speechless for a full minute and then he speaks out loudly, "What joy and new life to one who had 'walked on'. One who has been given back to us to love by Wakantanka. This night He has blessed the joining in marriage of our sons and daughters.

"This first powwow has the power to make all of us dakotas and let that be strong until there is no life from Mother Earth to give. Our people will now perform for you. Tomorrow go in peace and love and serve others, as you have been served. It is the Wish of Wakantanka and His Son, Tatanka Ska Son, that it be so. The Oglala Lakota will be lonely for your friendship until powwow after next winters cold winds blow away, may we know the warmth of our new dakotas once again."

Wanagiyata relates his father's words to all and then he leads the Oglala Lakota contingency of performers into the circle surrounding the big campfire. The three brother braves dance as if they were braves of many moons. They have secretly been taking lessons from Wachiwi (dancing Girl), Wanagiyata's new wife. Chief Matoskah is happy to sit and watch the show, once in a while, he will chant and his villagers cheer for him, for he is greatly loved by all Oglala Lakota. Part of the show features Wanagiyata, Oyaka, and Okolaya performing on their horses, shooting arrows and throwing spears and tomahawks at various targets with great skill, as they have been honing their skills with weapons, as all Oglala Lakota braves must do.

Next is a Wiwanyank Wacipi (the Sundance) performed by Wachiwi, dressed in her finest tahakalala (a buckskin dress) deer skin dress of light blue color, with white fringes and wearing huiyakaskes (ankle ornaments for Sundance – Lakota dialect) on her ankles and with her long black hair partially braided, with white and blue strips of taha (a deerskin) woven in each braid. She undoubtedly, is the most graceful and beautiful dancer ever seen by any tribes in attendance of the powwow.

Her parents and most especially her husband, Wanagiyata, are very proud of her skills and showmanship. Her dancing skills, gift from Wakantanka, to give in her own way, to all attending tribes of the powwow. To create joy is to give to Wakantanka's Children, and therefore it pleases Him. Always use your gifts whatever they may be, to glorify Wakantanka and His Son, Tatanka Ska Son. You will find your own tipi in

Mahpiya (Heaven, the clouds, the afterlife of mankind), and it will be big, beautiful, warm, comfortable and a never ending shelter just for caring for His Children.

All tribes are very pleased and the show is one of the best, most especially because of the bringing of life back to the daughter of Chief Bear Claw and Amitola. Wanagiyata's great miracle, with the help of Wakantanka and His Son, Tatanka Ska Son, will always be remembered at all Campfire Story Telling in the future by all tribes.

Until our next Campfire Story Telling – "New Powers New Missions," may Wakantanka be your guide in life's journey, with Him walking beside you; you will never be lost, only truly found.

Ḣoka

Chapter 7

New Powers New Missions

All the tribes attending their first powwow (a North American Indian gathering ceremony involving feasting, singing, dancing, and trading) given by the Oglala Lakota village of Chief Matoskah (white bear) are packing up and leaving for their own villages. The powwow the Oglala Lakota provided to their new dakotas (allies or friends), was a time of great miracles and fellowship and a chance to see and hear from Tatanka Ska Son (Son of Wakantanka) in person. This will be no doubt, for many, the greatest time in their lives on Mother Earth.

The alliances formed during this week of celebration and trading will keep the various tribes bonded together in the future, against any enemy that may come against any tribe attending the powwow. Next year's powwow should be even larger, if the Oglala Lakota want more to participate. Wanagiyata (in the land of spirits), Oyaka (to tell, report, relate), and Okolaya (to have as a friend), believe they can go on missions and unite many tribes to believe in Wakantanka (God) and His Son, Tatanka Ska Son. They will teach the values of the Oglala Lakota customs of fairness and respect for nature and their fellow human beings. They are all in reality, the Children of Wakantanka, making them brothers and sisters to all human beings on Mother Earth, who cares for all who love and respect her.

Chief Bagwungijik (hole in the sky – Chippewa dialect) of the Chippewa tribe is leaving at the head of his villagers, however, his daughter, Gidagaakoons (fawn – Chippewa dialect), remains with her new husband Oyaka, now a Oglala Lakota brave with new high standing. His standing is among all who know about him and his close bond with Wanagiyata 'The Great Healer' and their best friend Okolaya. The three 'Story Tellers' have the powers of speaking all dialects of any tribe. These 'special gifts' were given by Tatanka Ska Son to His 'Three Earthly Story Tellers'. One other, Crow Axxaashe Bachhee (Sun Man), has been given great strength to be used for good works for his people and their protection from enemy tribes.

The three 'Story Tellers' are on a fishing trip as spring has shown it's colors and sweet songs of nature's creatures abound and they have gone to their favorite fishing spot, not just for fish, but because Wanagiyata has asked for this time to speak with his brothers in Tatanka Ska Son. He has been praying for the Will of Wakantanka to be known to him and has received His answer and instructions. Those instructions include all three of Wakantanka's warriors and Wanagiyata is about to share the mission they will go on soon with his brothers.

Fishing has been good and even after they have eaten their fill in camp this night, there will be plenty to take back to their new wives and the parents of each warrior. To be enrolled in the service of Tatanka Ska Son is truly the highest of honors and any missions He sends them on will be performed, with the utmost dedication. Okolaya has pulled a skewer —made from a willow tree limb and stripped of all its bark, so it won't affect the taste of the fish— and loaded with campfire cooked hogleglega (the grass pike, or perhaps also, the rainbow fish) off a tripod cooking rack he has constructed from thick tree branches.

He serves his brothers hot rainbow trout and a soup he has made from beans, corn and peas. He has learned how to make this dish from his wife, the tall and beautiful Kimimila (butterfly), who is a great cook and missed greatly, she is his treasure. The great meal by chef Okolaya is shared with joy in the voices of each as the three brothers who have not had much private time alone with each other, since their recent marriages.

"My dear brothers, I have been praying to Wakantanka and His Wakan (holy – Lakota dialect) Nagi (a soul), the Holy Spirit has answered me with a vision in the night. We are to go to the village of Sun Man and enlist him in our mission and quest. Once he is with us, we will travel far to the northwest and touch the tribes there with the words of Wakantanka, as told by Tatanka Ska Son, who will advise and travel by our side each day of our lives," says Wanagiyata.

"What is our mission brother"? asked Oyaka. "While Chief Cougar Man (Ndolkan Homme – Apache dialect) of the Jicarilla

Apache (see appendix page 214) was at powwow, he asked me to come and tell many campfire stories to other Apache tribes. I told him, if Wakantanka deems it to be, it will be done. I also told Chief Cougar Man, he could be a 'Story Teller' for Tatanka Ska Son, until I could come and help him in this mission. He agreed with my words and promised to do so," said Wanagiyata.

Wanagiyata continues after a short pause, "My vision shows me another path, we will go to the big water of deep blue, where none from our tribe has ever journeyed. I was told in my night vision, there are people, speaking different words in more villages than there are fish in our fishing place and many more.

"We are to gather up our wives and Sun Man, of the Crow Nation, and go 'story telling' about the life Wakantanka has for us in Mahpiya (Heaven) forever, to as many tribes, as we can visit for two winters time. We may return to our Oglala Lakota village for powwow, only after this mission is done. We will have many new campfire stories to share with all who have gathered.

"Our mission is great and the weight of it must be born upon our spirits with love and honor to Wakantanka. Some of the tribes we are told to visit are the Chinook, Tillamook, Coast Salish Flathead and the Tlingit —many northwest Indians tribes we may visit in our mission— many of whom worship 'totem poles', which some men carve with axes and knives and lead their people in a false belief. We must have them believe in Wakantanka the only true God, for it is He only He, Who gives

130

life forever. That is our mission, and I am glad to do it."

The three brothers, as best friends, are very excited and anxious to go and the braves break camp in the early light and head back to their village. When they arrive, they are met by their wives and the welcome is warm and all who have been given rainbow trout are grateful. Each 'Story Teller' relates their plans to journey far away and for at least two winter's time, before they can return.

Oyaka's wife, Gidagaakoons, is concerned, that her parents Chief Bagwungijik and mother, Amitola (rainbow – Chippewa dialect), will be expecting a visit soon by the newlyweds. She is assured that Canška (red-legged hawk, the large white-breasted hawk, a snake eater), a friend of Oyaka and most dependable, has been asked by Oyaka to go and visit and explain, that their daughter will be safe with those who do Wakantanka's bidding. All the new wives are excited to be honored to go along with their husbands for this great adventure and for the opportunity to be with their husbands. They will be able to serve them and comfort them in their mission to the great northwest lands. In addition to, being able to see the great blue waters, no Oglala Lakota or Chippewa has ever beheld.

The three newlyweds, with wives and many šunkawakans (a horse) loaded down with supplies, some are pulling travois (a type of sledge) made from tipi (a teepee or tent or lodge) poles and are carrying tatanka (a male buffalo) skins for both warmth and to cover their tipis, set up when weather dictates, otherwise when weather is good, sleeping in the open under the stars, is a blessing few in a modern world will ever know, how sad.

Leading the way are four of the greatest scouts, to ever serve man. They are happy to serve their friends Oglala Lakota brothers. Both Mato Ḣota (a grizzly bear) Titakuye (immediate relatives) a grizzly bear brother and Šungmanitu (a wolf) Aitancan (the ruler over) and his two faithful šungmanitu scouts are eager to go and serve on this mission.

Wolf Ruler has assigned his best šungmanitu pack-member Long Tooth hehanhankeca (each so long – Lakota dialect) hiakigle (to set the teeth firmly – Lakota dialect), that he trusts to lead in his absence. Mato Ḣota Brother has only one responsibility and that will not keep him in his home of the woods. That huge responsibility is to his enormous stomach, which he fills every day without fail.

The 'Story Tellers' reach the outskirts of the Crow village of Sun Man. The first outer Crow guard on guard duty sees Mato Ḣota Brother and then Šungmanitu Ruler and realizes they are friends to each other and are traveling together in friendship, and that could only be the ones who were so admired and honored at powwow in the early spring. He saw them there and recognizes them and lets out a loud whoop and the entire village begins to buzz with excitement, as their great honored guests arrive.

There is a big celebration that night and many stories are told. Two villagers are brought to Wanagiyata by Sun Man who asked if he will heal them in the Name of Tatanka Ska Son. Wanagiyata prays and they are healed and all the Crow villagers are very impressed and great joy is shared by all. Sun Man is asked to join the mission to the northwest and agrees without hesitation. He feels his village is safe, as his reputation has spread far and wide, and no one would attack his people and live to tell that story by any campfire. Crow Chief Chogan (blackbird – Algonquin dialect) will miss Sun Man, who has made many improvements in the Crow villager's daily lives. He is thankful

132

that word of this powerful warrior has passed to many tribes, insuring that no enemy tribes would come against them.

Mission members completed, a good night's rest is enjoyed and Wachiwi (dancing girl), Gidagaakoons and Kimimila have had a great visit with some of the Crow women they met at powwow and trade for some items, they may need in their travels. Sun Man packs his horse and is given another to pack his supplies. His horse is in beautiful condition, her coat shines, and her muscles stand out in full definition, outlining her great strength and running ability. However, he is still not able to out run his master, the great and powerful Crow Sun Man, so blessed by Wakantanka.

Mid-day finds the uniquely qualified mission members are attempting a crossing of a river of fast water, when two of the šunkawakans carrying tatanka hides try to cross to the other river bank; they are swept downriver and are screaming loud whinnies. Sun Man springs into action and swims like a ptan (the otter – Lakota dialect). He grabs both horses by their

šunkawakan tawanap'in (a horse collar) and pulls them to the far side of the bank to safety. Then he helps all across safely, including Šungmanitu Ruler. Mato Hota Brother, needs no such help, he has had many swimming lessons with slippery rainbow trout and passed every swim test above, as well as under water, pursuing them with great skill.

When all are safely on the other side of the cold river, everyone and the tatanka hides are wet, so camp is made and the tipis are set up, fires are made and everything is being dried out. It is hard work, and everyone is glad for resting in camp a day and another night, before they renew their journey. High mountains lay before them and scouting must be done, before a final route is taken.

The next night in camp, preparing to choose a route over the mountains spread out before them, Wanagiyata is reminded of his flight in the high mountains on the big white furry back of Tatanka Ska Son. He tells this story about meeting and flying upon the back of Tatanka Ska Son with his brothers before they were braves and adolescent Oglala Lakota boys. Sun Man is enthralled by this story and asked Wanagiyata, "We could sure use His powers to get us over and through these big mountain passes loaded with snow, but I can't fly, can you Wanagiyata"?

Suddenly the sky lights up the early night darkness and ablaze in blue light, Tatanka Ska Son flies in and lands in camp

 and all including the great waowešica (a bear in general) Mato Ȟota Brother and Šungmanitu Ruler bow down in reverence and honor the Son of Wakantanka. Tatanka Ska Son speaks, "Rise up and know that I am with you. I will stay the night and when the morning light comes, We will fly among the mountains, so you will know your way among My Father's beautiful creations, where many eagles fly. Sun Man, you will fly with My 'Chosen Ones', for you have been 'chosen' to serve also, by Wakantanka, My Father, who lives high in the heavens

and has already giving you the gift of great strength.

All in the Oglala Lakota and Crow camp were excited to have Tatanka Ska Son in their camp and with the promise to fly among the eagles high in the mountains. Morning, finds a fresh pile of hogleglega lying near the campfire kept in life and ready to be used to cook a fine fresh morning meal. What a thoughtful act by the powers of Tatanka Ska Son, who needs no food or substance in a human world.

After early meal, all the braves load up for a flight upon the broad back of Tatanka Ska Son while the wonderful new brides, who serve in love and devotion, make ready all for travel breaking camp and loading the šunkawakans. Lift off is slow and easy, with all taking a strong grip on the beautiful white fur of Tatanka Ska Son.

Soon many eagles surround them, feeling the special presences of the Son of Wakantanka and His Spirit, which most of Mother Earth's creatures feel, —even before humans, which is evident,  when earthquakes and other natural disaster threaten, God's creatures are first to sense and know mysteriously that they are coming— and fly side by side in a way of honoring Tatanka Ska Son and His presence among them deep in the ska (white – Lakota dialect) mahpihpiya (scattering clouds – Lakota dialect).

All of Mother Earth's creatures love and respect their creator Wakantanka and His Son, Tatanka Ska Son, and recognize His presence at all times. When wicaša (a man) feel the lack of the presence of the Wakan (holy) Nagi (spirit), they will always be very lonely. Mother Earth is never alone when Wakantanka is with them, as His Spirit dwells within all of Mother Earth's creatures. They were created to serve man as food or in labor, and will be in His kingdom whenever they 'walk on'. Wakantanka has made this so, that they may be with Him always, as they are innocent in His eyes and He loves them all.

Wanagiyata is watching closely as they fly through various mountain passes and makes a mental note of the shortest route through traveling northwest. Sun Man is feeling so blessed once again with the gift, Tatanka Ska Son has given him and with this wonderful opportunity to fly like the anunkasan (bald eagle – Lakota dialect). Sun Man knows this special gift is only for those He has chosen to fly with Him before, and he is with all of them now. He also, tries to remember the passes he has been shown by Tatanka Ska Son on this magical flight high in the mountains bearing heavy white heads of snow.

Okolaya, loses his grip, when Tatanka Ska Son, makes a sharp turn to miss an outcropping of a high mountain peak and falls off screaming for help. Tatanka Ska Son shouts, "Hold on tight My 'Story Tellers', We are in a rescue mission." He dives, in a thunderous dive, not unlike a bolt of lightning, down and almost instantly catches up with the falling Okolaya and flies under him. Which enables Okolaya to once again grab on and seat himself, behind all the passengers riding on Tatanka Ska Son's, broad ska fury back, once again in complete comfort and safety. Wow, that was quite an experience for Okolaya, much like falling off a high cliff and being saved from certain death, almost like an eagle catching a fish which is jumping in midair.

Tatanka Ska Son circles over the mountains retracing His previous flight path; to refresh the memories of His passengers of the route they should take in their mission to spread the Words of His Father, Wakantanka, to many tribes in the northwest. Tatanka Ska Son lands in camp and bids the braves unload from His tall back, then to everyone's great surprise, He invites Wachiwi, Gidagaakoons, and Kimimila to get aboard. He wants to give them the gift of flight, as no other women in the world have ever experienced, and further to help them understand the blessings He has given to their husbands and to know their most important standing with Him. The new wives drop the reins of all the šunkawakans and rush to mount upon the Son of God, Tatanka Ska Son, not needing a second invitation for this great honor and gift for surely, the highest of adventure of their young lives.

While Tatanka Ska Son is flying the wives around over the mountains, Wanagiyata, pulls a soft taha (a deerskin) skin from his šunkawakan's (a horse) wak'inpi (a pack – Lakota dialect) and marks what he has remembered about the route to take, on a deerskin with a sharp stick he rubs with ashes from his campfire to draw a crude map. All the mission party are completing preparations to travel and are ready to go once their wives land with many stories to be told, among other women of other villages they will visit. When Tatanka Ska Son touches anyone's heart, they will almost always, become a 'Story Teller'.

Soon the women land and dismount from the broad back of Tatanka Ska Son and thank Him for the great gift of flying on His broad back through the mountains high among the ska clouds. Tatanka Ska Son says, "Go now and serve My Children, tell them of My Father's love for them and, I Am That I Am, and they should believe in Me." Tatanka Ska Son slowly lifts off and disappears into the clouds that are forming in the deep blue sky.

It looks like a storm could be brewing. Wanagiyata, urges everyone to make haste to reach further up into the mountain pass lying before them. It is late in the day and they have made good progress. Luckily —no luck, only the guidance of Tatanka Ska Son— Šungmanitu Ruler has located a cave entrance near to the path the 'Story Tellers' have been traveling. He enters with Mato Ḣota Brother, right behind him to scout for danger and any other details; they can give their leader, Wanagiyata, when they report back to him.

The cave has a mother waonze (a nickname for a sakehanska, the grizzly bear – Lakota dialect) and her mato cincala (bear cub – Lakota dialect). Mato Ḣota Brother gently wakes her from her sleep and ask her to move to the rear of the cave and not to be afraid. He tells her that she and her baby waowešica (a bear in general) will be safe. They will be fed a meal, —momma bear

gets deer meat, baby mato cincala will have her mother's rich milk— before they go back to a long sleep for the rest of the long winter. Baby bear loved the attention he got from all the female Indian women and the two šungmanitu scouts, who love to romp and play with any young things, animal or human.

A great storm is starting to throw her powerful winds carrying heavy snowflakes at all the 'Story Tellers' in the mountainous area. Šungmanitu Ruler leaves Mato Hota Brother with his new female friend and her cub and runs to lead Wanagiyata and the mission party to the safety of the cave. Once again, unknowingly, Tatanka Ska Son has provided safety for His 'Chosen Ones'.

The great blizzard lasts for three days and drops snow to the height of the chest of a tall šunkawakan. It would have been very hard to stay warm in a tipi during this great powerful storm, much less of a chance to shelter the horses. The mother mato hota and her cub have joined the group and have enjoyed food and a warm fire and true friendship with these special beings. After this fellowship, they will never attack a human being, unless attacked first.

After the storm has passed, the great sun brings her warmth and starts to melt the heavy over-burden of snow; there is a clearing of most of the snow, to a manageable depth in which to travel by horseback. Flooding is taking place in the lower altitudes. They are fortunate to be above the flooding, by way of the expert scouting by Šungmanitu Ruler and his two extra šungmanitu scouts. Finding passages that are not flooded, as the mission party travel through two passages and make it part way though the mountain range before them in a time span of four long days duration.

One valley they have reached has a small contingent of Assiniboine, Ojibwe Asiniibwaan ("stone Sioux") Indians. Their village is near a mountain stream in —now current Southern Montana area. The village is approached very slowly by Wanagiyata. He has decided to ride Mato Hota Brother and meet their outer guard and have him go into the village to announce their arrival.

When Wanagiyata gets within hearing range, he hears the guards talk when they switch guard duty and Wanagiyata knows their dialect and then he says in the Assiniboine dialect, "Be not afraid, I come with empty hands, in peace. When you see me, you will know by that which I ride, that I come in peace along with and my brother bear. I come to visit your people and share a great campfire story. Go and summon your chief, as I would speak with him, before I come forward," says Wanagiyata.

The outer guard jumps to the ready at the first words coming from the trees nearby, he is frighten as the words of Wanagiyata come through loud and clear. How this stranger speaks his tongue, is unknown to him, this stranger is not a tribal member. He calls for another Assiniboine brave to come and then to take the news to Chief Crazy Bear (Mahtowitko – Assiniboine dialect), that a stranger has come. He is chief of the small band of less than one hundred villagers.

Chief Crazy Bear brings four of his warriors with him, when he slowly approaches Wanagiyata and is completely amazed by what he sees. Never has he or any of his people seen a man ride a huge brown grizzly bear. He and his braves go to a kneeling position, as they believe this strange Indian brave to be of a holy origin. His own braves think he may be a relative of their chief, he who rides a great bear. This is the thought of many because of their Assiniboine chief's own name, Crazy Bear.

Wanagiyata riding on Mato Hota Brother, slowly approach to within ten feet of the kneeling Assiniboine's. "I come as a friend and dakota with my brother the great grizzly bear," says Wanagiyata, knowing what tribe of people he is speaking to. Chief Crazy Bear, hears the words, but does not understand the Oglala Lakota dialect he has heard, so he tries to sign and the says in his dialect, 'I am Chief Crazy Bear of the Nakoda Oyadebi (Assiniboine Nakoda Nation), you are welcome in our village'.

Wanagiyata knows his dialect and repeats his words first spoken in his dialect to Chief Crazy Bear in his dialect. The chief and his braves are even more surprised by this strange Indian brave and his unnatural powers. "Rise up, Chief Crazy Bear; I have come with my brothers and their wives, to tell a wonderful campfire story given to me by our God, Wakantanka. He has asked me to tell you and your people of His love and to help you believe in Him and His Son, Tatanka Ska Son.

I have many great stories to tell and so do my companions, some of which you will be surprised, are friends to us, and travel as guides and scouts, be not afraid, as they show themselves to you. Wait until my family and friends who travel with me come before you to be seen," says Wanagiyata in the early western Siouan language.

As the remainder of the 'Story Tellers' arrive and line up facing Chief Crazy Bear and his braves, their eyes widen when each see the friendly wolves and beautiful wives of the Oglala Lakota Nation. Wanagiyata speaks up in the Assiniboine dialect, "Please stand, to be our friend." Now Oyaka and Okolaya understand the dialect they need to speak with the Assiniboine of this small village by the cold waters of a beautiful mountain stream.

Chief Crazy Bear stands and steps toward Wanagiyata and Wanagiyata moves toward him and shows his palms up and they are empty, they carry no weapons, but the smile on his face carries a message of trust and friendship. Chief Crazy Bear speaks up, "You are most welcome, come and share of food and humble lodges if you need them." Everyone follows the Hunga (tribal chief – Assiniboine dialect) and his braves, as they enter their village of lodges made of willow branches in a conical shape, covered by tabloka (a buck, the male of the common deer – Lakota dialect), hehaka (male elk) and heton (horned – Lakota dialect) cik'ala (antelope – Lakota dialect) hides.

All the villagers are standing frozen in amazement at the sight of these strange visitors, but are made at ease as their chief speaks out about them as friends, who should be welcome. Soon the village is buzzing with cooking, as the Assiniboine women, heat round river rocks and then places them in cooking pots to boil meat and roast buffalo meat and cook dried nuts and berries in a sauce. There will be a meeting of other hungabi (little chiefs – Assiniboine dialect) about their special visitors. After this meeting of little chiefs, all is decided, to open all hospitality their village can give to Wanagiyata this night and all nights until they leave.

The chief and his Assiniboine villagers are wonderful people, very free in their attitudes and thinking, which is a good thing, as they are open to listen to the 'Story

Tellers' and many will believe in Wakantanka and His Son, Tatanka Ska Son. All the children have taken up with the wild creatures, they have always feared. Mato Hota Brother is surrounded by many and some climb on him as he lies by one of many campfires. Šungmanitu Ruler and his two faithful šungmanitu scouts have been adopted by many young boys and are being fed dried buffalo jerky. It is a joyous time. On the second night, Chief Crazy Bear calls all the villagers together and introduces, Wanagiyata to speak and tell his many campfire stories, which he does in their language.

He tells the story of the two Earths, the Earlier Earth and this Earth, Mother Earth, which all life now lives on in His great love. It is a story that is so astounding, that many are dumb struck with total silence, not to miss one word from this special one, who walks in the land of spirits. Many have heard the words of Wanagiyata.

Now many more hear Oyaka and Okolaya as they speak and visit all the lodges and teach through their own personal stories; also they speak of their experiences with Tatanka Ska Son and what they have done in many wars and their personal witness to healings they have seen performed by Tatanka Ska Son, and Wanagiyata.

The Oglala Lakota women and new brides blend in well and help the Assiniboine Indian women showing them some new cooking skills, which are a big hit. Some small trading is done and it is a great time of celebration shared by all in this new exciting friendship and learning each is experiencing.

The Oglala Lakota have setup their own tipis and have shown their host how to construct these handy and warm lodges, which can be easily transported and they shed the rain and snow in a most efficient manner due to their sharp angular shape. Gidagaakoons has shown many of the women how to make cooking bowls and other cooking items, while Wachiwi teaches various dances and shows many how to weave and sew in her way. Kimimila has many talents to share and helps Chief Crazy Bear's wife with her varied knowledge learned from her dear departed mother. Some cooking instructions, involve the use of certain spices, all new to the Assiniboine.

Kimimila has developed a mix of spices that enhances the taste of a bland food diet, and it is readily taken to by all who taste this spiced food for the first time. Much is learned and many hours of visitation are passed in many different lodges, as a week passes, before Wanagiyata announces that they must depart and continue their mission to the far northwestern tribal villages he plans to visit.

They will leave in the morning, but not without first inviting the Assiniboine village to travel east in early spring, to join the Oglala Lakota villagers and others tribes in hosting their great powwow. Wanagiyata tells Chief Crazy Bear to give a message to Chief Matoskah his father that he was given the invitation to join the powwow by his son, Wanagiyata and to extend a warm welcome. Wanagiyata leaves Chief Crazy Bear a crude, but concise map of how to reach the Oglala Lakota village.

Chief Crazy Bear is very excited, about this invitation and so are his people, when they are told about this great powwow and what it means to them in many ways. They will all start to make various items to trade and make everything ready which they will need for travel, including the new tipis that they have learned to make. Hunting, fishing and all food preparation will be in full swing within a week's time, if Chief Crazy Bear has his way after the Oglala Lakota have moved on to the northwest.

It is very quiet in the semi-darkness, as a soft snow falls on the village just as the sun is raising, and a loud warning is heard coming from the outside agicida (soldier; camp watcher – Assiniboine dialect) on duty, as he runs in to warn the village of an incoming attack, by far ranging Apache raiders. Sun Man, who has not shown his great strength to any of these people, although some have been told of his gift of great strength from Wakantanka, who is soundly asleep. He is awakened immediately by the yelling, grabs his great stone wicat'e (an instrument with which to kill) and charges out to meet about one hundred and fifty Apache warriors.

He has slain at least seventy, before Wanagiyata, Oyaka, Okolaya, Mato Hota Brother, Šungmanitu Ruler and his scouts, all face off with the enemy attackers. They kill many more and route the remaining twenty surviving Apache enemy, who have seen the power of this foe, a mix of great warriors, a mighty warrior with a stone club, no one can defeat and ferocious animals warriors.

All the Jicarilla Apache retreat in great haste, leaving their wounded behind, which is cowardice, but great fear has gripped them. Some Assiniboine village warriors, along with the village agicida have been badly wounded in the terrible hand to hand battle. Chief Crazy Bear has been wounded by an Apache arrow, which has pierced deep into his right shoulder, and he goes down in pain to his knees. He sees all the visitors have rallied to save

145

his village, along with the personal opportunity to witness of the great strength he had heard about, seeing with his own eyes, the great and powerful Sun Man of the Crow Nation in action.

The entire village is alive with response to the attacking Apache; many braves gather up the wounded Apache and take them prisoner. Wanagiyata and Sun Man carry Chief Crazy Bear to his lodge, where his wife moves to help with his wound. Wanagiyata starts to pray by his side and soon the warmth of healing power surges thought his being.

He tells Chief Crazy Bear to relax and that he will feel no pain. Then he grabs the Apache arrow and pulls it slowly out and the wound closes and he is completely healed. Chief Crazy Bear is astounded by this miracle, and follows Wanagiyata out of his lodge. Next, Wanagiyata goes to the aid of other wounded Assiniboine and heals them. Then with Chief Crazy Bear now by his side, he visits the wounded Apache raiders being held prisoner and heals them all, however he does not order them freed.

He asked Chief Crazy Bear to free them, showing them his great mercy, as he knows they will be a walking, talking witnesses to their tribal villagers, when they return home. He further explains that is the Will of Wakantanka. Chief Crazy Bear readily agrees with the wise counsel of Wanagiyata and tells the healed Apache raiders, who are in total disbelief of all that has happened in their favor, to go in peace.

The Great Chief Crazy Bear is highly respected by his

warriors, for his wisdom and mercy. The Apache, do not know Sun Man is not one of the Assiniboine tribe and the story will be told, do not attack the Assiniboine living here, or death may surely find you. They are given rations of food and escorted out of the village and they head back south to their village far away.

Many are very happy at the great victory and the healing of the wounded and healing of their chief and now seeing Wanagiyata's power of healing, many come forward, who have some small old injuries and other health issues. Some with bad teeth also come forward. Wanagiyata heals them all. The Oglala Lakota and great and powerful Crow Sun Man are not allowed to leave, not without one last celebration of thanksgiving, it has been a great victory and the Assiniboine village has been saved from the fierce Apache raiders. The friendship and risking of lives, given here by all the visitors, is a treasure for all the Assiniboine Indian village to pass on at future campfire 'Story Telling' and they plan to do so, at powwow next year, with all their new dakotas.

The next day all gather around the wonderful new friends and dakotas, as they filed out of their village led by Šungmanitu Ruler and his šungmanitu scouts, who immediately fan out left and right of the column. Mato Ḣota Brother has five young Indian boys laughing as they ride on his broad back and as they jump off just out of camp. Mato Ḣota Brother, turns around, stands up high on his back legs and waves farewell to the Assiniboine villagers and growls deeply many times in a friendly farewell manner.

Until our next Campfire Story Telling – "Rafting Up The Great River," may Wakantanka be with you and bless all your good deeds done in His Precious Name.

Lakota Chief Red Horse

Chief Red Horse (1822, Nebraska – 1907, Cheyenne River Indian Reservation, South Dakota) was a sub-chief of the Miniconjou Sioux. He fought in the Battle of the Little Bighorn, in 1881, he gave one of the few detailed accountings of the event. He also drew pictographs of the Little Bighorn Battle. Red Horse married twice and had three children. -Wikipedia

Chapter 8

Rafting Up The Great River

The visit with the Assiniboine village was very fulfilling to our 'Story Tellers'. Many became believers and will join all believers in Mahpiya (Heaven), after life's breath is replaced by the cold chill of death, which those who believe, will never feel. Absent from the body, present with Wakantanka (God) and His Son, Tatanka Ska Son (Son of Wakantanka), which is His promise to all mankind. Something very important, that will help greatly in the journey of our 'Story Tellers' to the northwest country, was shared with Wanagiyata (in the land of spirits) by Assiniboine Chief Mahtowitko (Crazy Bear – Assiniboine dialect), before Wanagiyata left the small village.

Chief Crazy Bear told Wanagiyata, that there was a great river south of his village five days travel on foot. This river leads far away to the west, further than any of his people had ever traveled and returned to tell the story of its ending. He did not know if it was a good way to travel, if one had canoes or a log raft to carry them on the great waters flowing east. It would be a fight against the current, when the water ran fast in narrow places, otherwise, it could be traveled, but not without danger and hardship at times along its westward route.

Wanagiyata, prayed about this way to travel his last night among the Assiniboine people and when he awoke, he made a decision to head south and find this river, which might bring his mission to other tribes, who may live along its banks. Before leaving with the 'Story Tellers', he trades with Chief Crazy Bear's tribe for all the rope made from animal skins and any animal skins he could trade for and loaded on his iwaglamnas (an extra or fresh horse) and headed south by southwest.

This trip would be easier and faster with his beloved šunkawakans (a horse) and Wanagiyata calculated the mission party of 'Story Tellers' should find the Great River within a few days. The terrain travel toward the Great River was through dense forest trees and over and through some mountain passes. Led by the faithful lead scout Šungmanitu (a wolf) Aitancan (the ruler over) and his two šungmanitu scouts running out to the left and right, speaking in wolf language, directing Wanagiyata in a better way, if he was not aware of another path of travel. This practice was very efficient and saved time and hardship in many cases along the journey of the 'Story Tellers' by horseback.

Wanagiyata is leading, with Oyaka (to tell, report, relate) riding behind him leading three šunkawakans. Behind him are the three new brides, Wachiwi (dancing Girl), Gidagaakoons (fawn – Chippewa dialect) and Kimimila (butterfly), each leading one loaded down šunkawakan. Behind them is the great powerful Sun Man of the Crow Nation, and he is leading all the remaining ten horses, tied together and in tow behind him.

Bringing up the rear-guard position is, Okolaya (to have as a friend), who is keeping a good eye on everything in front, side to side and to the rear, for any threat or danger. The huge mato hota (grizzly bear), Mato Hota Titakuye (the immediate relatives) Grizzly Brother is following behind Wolf Ruler, and never seems tired, but always seems hungry. He snacks on whatever he can grab during his travel and stuff into his great mouth.

There are animals here in the deep woods of northwest that have never seen a šunkawakan, much less a human being riding  them. Okolaya has dropped back a little distance from the last string of horses Sun Man is leading, after he sensed something that seemed out of order and it was troubling him, so he was very alert. The 'Story Tellers' were strung out and were serpentine in there way of travel, around large boulders and up and down they went, as they were led by their wolf scouts. Just as Okolaya was coming around a large boulder, a big heavy male igmuwatogla (mountain lion – Lakota dialect) slammed into him, knocking him off his horse, which also was taken off his feet by the impact of the attacking mountain lion. Okolaya's horse whinnied in a screaming loud sound, as he rolled over.

Okolaya is locked in deadly combat, battling for his life with the mountain lion and has his left forearm in the mouth of the mountain lion and has pulled his knife. He is attempting to stab the mountain lion, which is clawing him with his left paw and his long claws are ripping at Okolaya's chest and neck, inflicting long deep cuts. He is bleeding badly, as he stabs the mountain lion in the ribs, whenever he can get a clear angle to thrust his knife between the left clawing paw of this savage and powerful mountain lion.

His first stab hits a rib and does not go in deep and glances off. Now, the mountain lion moves his left paw and pins Okolaya's right arm down and tries to shake his head and releases his bite and frees his mouth from Okolaya's left arm, in order that he can try to bite his face or neck for a final killing bite from his powerful jaws. Silently, Okolaya is praying to Wakantanka for help and believes he will die; he is already bleeding to death at this point in the mountain lion attack.

Suddenly, the huge heavy mountain lion is pulled off Okolaya, by powerful hands, by the neck and his jaws are grabbed by the hands of Sun Man and he pulls the mountain lion's jaws apart. A loud cracking sound is heard and the mountain lion goes limp as his life has been ended by Sun Man's incredible strength. Okolaya is passing out from his loss of blood and his eyes roll back in his head. Sun Man scoops him up and runs like a heton cik'ala (a horned antelope) heading to the front of the column, toward Wanagiyata.

As he passes by the wives, Kimimila sees him and screams

out in horror, jumps from her horse, dropping her reins and the lead-line of her pack horse and runs after Sun Man and her wounded new husband limp in his powerful arms. As she runs, she is thinking of how she loves him so deeply, that if she loses him, after the great loss of her parents, her heart will not heal again. This is the thought in her mind when she reaches her husband's side.

Okolaya is unconscious and covered with blood. Wanagiyata is praying beside him, as is Sun Man. Okolaya moans and his

eyes open and his wounds close slowly and bleeding is stopped. His body is covered in blood and it begins to disappear, soon the blood on Sun Man begins to disappear. Wakantanka has answered the prayers of His 'Story Tellers'. Now all give thanks and praise to their God, Wakantanka, and His Son, Tatanka Ska Son. Tatanka Ska Son was watching over them, but let this attack and following miracle take place, as it has further bonded the entire 'Story Tellers' even deeper than before, with the threat of losing one so loved by all.

Sun Man chases down both horses that have been spooked and brings them back to Kimimila. Meanwhile, Wanagiyata goes to the dead mountain lion field dresses and skins him and feeds all his friends of the woods. The rest of the mission members, rest before starting their journey again with great thankfulness in their hearts for the life of Okolaya. Great joy is in the air and Mato Hota Brother has a very big belly and smile on his face.

It is a good day to keep traveling and many more miles are put behind them before they stop and make camp near a fast-moving mountain stream. All the horses are tethered (tie an animal with rope or chain so as to restrict its movement) in a meadow and have been unloaded and rubbed down after being washed. Their care is paramount for all, most especially for Sun Man's horse, which he has named Xapáaliia (Baaxpeé which means "power transcending the ordinary." The physical manifestation of Baaxpeé is Xapáaliia, often referred to as 'medicine', which represents and acts as a conduit of Baaxpeé given to a Crow by God – Crow dialect – Wikipedia).

If Sun Man does not honor Wakantanka by taking care of his horse with his own hand, he will lose his great strength. No human knows this secret, but him and Wakantanka. She always gets extra special care at all times and it sets a good example to all who own or care for a šunkawakan.

The young wives, cook a fine meal of roasted hehaka (the male elk), that Šungmanitu Ruler hunted down and his powerful friend, Mato Hota Brother carried back to camp in his strong jaws, for the braves to clean and the women to cook. The rest of the meat will be dried and stored for their journey west. All the animal brothers are still full of a big mountain lion, which choose the wrong prey to attack and now as all animals who give their life, live in Mahpiya (Heaven) as a peaceful life is given to them, to serve Wakantanka in a loving way. Kimimila serves her brave husband his meal with special kindness and grace that a truly strong loving wife can only give, thankful that she is able to do so, for she thought he may have been lost to her in this life.

The next morning's sun, finds our 'Story Tellers' once again strung-out in a long column, as they slowly make their way west by southwest in search of the mighty Great River. Which they have been told, may make their journey easier and provide a chance to come in contact with more tribes to teach and spread the Words of Wakantanka and His love for them. Think about how wonderful it is to be a 'Story Teller' responsible for saving the soul and spirit of others, gifting them with life forever, because only the physical body dies, but the soul and its spirit never dies.

The difference is without believing in Wakantanka and His Son, Tatanka Ska Son, your soul will wonder among the evil ones gone before. Those whom are all lost from the presence of Wakantanka forever, and suffer a never ending damnation of loneliness. The pain of many forest fires, no waters can quench, because there is no water or anything of use that can relieve this suffering they all share. How can anyone choose not to believe in the Creator of all, Wakantanka the God of love? Only those who choose lust, and evil deeds through selfishness, will be lost in their mean ways and disservice toward Wakantanka's Children. Always be kind and merciful, to all of Wakantanka's Creation. That is the path to follow in this short life's journey.

Many miles have been traveled and the beauty of this land is a sight that fills one's spirit with wonder and appreciation for the gift of life and the chance to live it fully, in the company of family and friends. To live among the animals and hear their songs, to see the stars at night and hear the night sounds and feel safe in your blanket, knowing Wakantanka is with you. This is the life the 'Story Tellers' are living, a life in the arms of 'Mother Earth', serving Wakantanka and His Son, Tatanka Ska Son. It is the best life one can live, a life of service and all the 'Story Tellers' are living it to the fullest.

Wanagiyata, has been thinking this, as he follows the trail breakers, Šungmanitu Ruler and his two šungmanitu scouts, who he has given the names of Akita One (to seek or hunt for, as something lost – Lakota dialect) and Akita Two. He now turns his mind to the progress they have made and believes; that they may reach the Great River sometime in tomorrow's sun, before the shadow of trees elongate themselves upon the earth and cross over her waters, before they see her. It will be as it will be, as God (Wakantanka) has planned.

Camp is made and Wanagiyata explains to all, that he believes what Chief Crazy Bear has said about the great river, leading to the west should be near. Everyone is excited to reach the Great River. The new wives begin cooking, as the men care for all horses and secure and protect the supplies they carry. After being served their late meal by their new wives, the braves once again decide who will serve as night guard first and who will take the remaining watches.

Okolaya is first to go on night guard, all others sleep in their blankets, under the stars near a campfire. This is all shared and whoever is on guard duty, keeps it fed with wood stored nearby. This is a good system and insures the comfort of all in the colder night air throughout the entire night and keeps the campfire ready to cook on in the early morning. This practice saves time before departure. He makes constant rounds around the camp, being very quiet, as not to disturb anyone, but most importantly to not give up his position, in case an enemy is trying to sneak in on the camp.

One must be still and stay alert at all times to be a great night guard, all lives in camp may depend on him and him alone. He has a big responsibility and he is vigil in his duties. To be caught sleeping on duty is severely punished by most tribes, many times death is the result required by many tribal laws they live by.

Okolaya is very diligent in his duties, as are all in this camp who serve as night guard.

It was a cold night and the smell of cooked elk meat roasted over the fire by Kimimila, who loves to cook and serve her husband and those she loves. The braves are brought out of their warm blankets by the aroma of food, which has already set Mato Hota Brother off to hunt for food, before Kimimila started cooking the raw elk meat.

The animal friends, who serve in this mission, have bonded and work together in many ways, one is to hunt together and that is very wise and works very well. Šungmanitu Ruler and Akita One and Akita Two are faster runners than Mato Hota Brother — although he can run thirty miles in one hour— so they spot, chase down and circle prey until he arrives and puts an end to the prey swiftly, with one swipe of his big powerful paw to the head.

Mato Hota Brother does not want those who give him life's food to suffer unnecessarily. This early morning finds the animal hunting team feeding on a large elk, when they are full in the stomach, they leave the rest of their meal to šunkmanitus (coyotes), who have been waiting impatiently, barking and yipping for a share of this meal.

With the early meal served and eaten, and camp broken down, with pack horses loaded and ready to travel, Wanagiyata is pleased to see his scouts ready to go on point. They show up eager to lead off on their journey westward and Wanagiyata gives the order to move out. The 'Story Tellers' have reached the top of a long tall hill and Wanagiyata is first to see down the other side, and he sees a wide body of clean water, it is the Great River. He thanks Wakantanka, that they have found this travel route, as Chief Crazy Bear has suggested and are safely nearing her shores. In one hour, they reach the north shore and Wanagiyata, tells everyone to set up the tipis (teepee or tent or lodge) and make a permanent camp for now. They will be here until a raft can be constructed and all made ready to travel by river. Everyone gets to work, except our scouts, who are on guard and resting, with their keen ears listening for any danger.

Camp has been made, complete with tipis and all supplies stored in one tipi. The šunkawakans have been tethered in a nearby open grass area, cleared of trees, by a wild fire and now supporting grass, as Mother Earth repairs her scared lands as needed. Akita Two, has been assigned to guard them, and is glad to do it.

The sun is setting upriver to the camp, as all in camp are eating their evening meal. Wanagiyata finishes eating and stands and says, "This is my plan; we will make a large raft from the logs of lighter trees, like the spruce tree. We will chop them down and then strip the bark off and let them dry out as we put them together on land. Then we can seal them with tallow and animal fat, which we must render.

"Sun Man is very strong and can gather and move many logs to our building site, where he will cut them to the size we need. We will need a raft that can carry seven with all supplies and give us cover from rain and cold. I will draw my picture of the raft and its' size tonight in my wife's tipi and we will study it in the morning, before we begin to make this new water lodge to shelter in, when needed."

Sun Man asks, "How will we go against the water, which moves to the east away from where we journey"? Wanagiyata answers, "My plan is to make a large paddle to steer the raft and keep it off shore, and have our šunkawakans pull our raft upstream against the slow moving waters, this way we all travel

together." Sun Man says, "It is a good plan and I am ready to make this plan live."

Everyone heads for their tipis, for much needed sleep, feeling safe with Mato Hota Brother, Šungmanitu Ruler, Akita One

guarding camp and Akita Two and Sun Man guarding the tethered šunkawakans nearby. Night sounds fill the night, with no winds blowing and lull all to sleep, except animal scouts, and those on night guard duty. They are keen to odd sounds, which warn of possible danger, some sleep with one eye open and both ears listening.

Early morning sunrise, finds Sun Man checking on his horse and giving her a rub down and checking her hooves for any sign of damage or cracks. He rubs some fatty oil he has concocted to keep his horse's feet in good condition. Wanagiyata has noticed how well Sun Man cares for his horse and likes this treatment and now all the horses get this care. After Sun Man finishes his care of his horse, he reports back to camp and enjoys a fine meal, from Kimimila's cooking pot. He is especially fond of her, and considers all the wives, sisters that he never had. After early meal, all gather around to see the drawing plan Wanagiyata has made for his raft design.

He explains his drawing to all and asks for any suggestions or changes, from anyone. First, needed for construction, is eight logs to be cut to a length of eleven arm lengths (approximately twenty-two feet), and the float-logs (logs that carry the weight of the raft floating directly in the water) will need to be from fingertip to elbow across the cut ends (eighteen inches thick). He explains further in his plan, they will need eight of these float logs and four additional logs seven arm lengths (fourteen feet long) and as thick as your upper leg (eight inches thick), to be used as cross connecting logs, which will be running across the float logs, two at the front and two at the back, which will bind all the float logs together creating the body of the raft.

A steering-pole will be needed, made of, a spread hand's length by eight arm lengths (six inch-thick by sixteen-feet long), then a large tree will be cut down and a flat piece of wood as large as your fist by two arm lengths long (four inches thick by four-feet long), will be cut off and a flat paddle shape carved from it. This paddle shaped piece will be attached to the steering pole at one end, creating a rudder to steer the raft. The steering pole will be placed between two, two arm lengths long by one upper leg thickness (four-feet long by eight-inch thick logs), which will be tied to the rear section of the raft, in an upward position and spaced about wrist to elbow length (ten inches) apart. They will be used as keeps (stops), for the steering pole to rest between and control the movement of the steering pole.

Sun Man and Wanagiyata go out among the forest and select the trees Wanagiyata needs to build the raft. Even with the great

160

strength of his mighty arms, Sun Man can only chop as hard as his stone-hatchet can be used with care not to break it. Wanagiyata selects all the trees and marks them, while Sun Man brings down the first tree. It is slow going, but he is able to bring two logs a day cut to the correct length to the building site.

The logs are placed on two other short logs off the ground and Oyaka and Okolaya strip the logs of their bark by chopping cuts every length of a spread hand (six inches) with their stone axes. Then using the sharp edge of their tomahawks (Algonquian name for a light ax – Algonquian dialect) to pry the bark off. It is hard work, but everyone is glad to do it.

The women are hard at work making ropes from the extra hides of deer and elk skin. They are needed to bind the logs together and make long lines to attach to the šunkawakans. This will make it possible to pull the raft attached to their harnesses, which they also have to make with help from the braves who are familiar with working with the horses.

There is much to do before they can once again begin their journey to the northwest and it will take time. However, to be prepared is the best way to journey, because it is harder to repair or replace any equipment on the move or in an emergency situation. Anytime you are on water, moving or still, you must be ready for trouble. Because only your water craft —as it may be— is all that is between you and being in the water. Where cold and current can take your life away and many have gone that way, because of poor planning and bad judgment.

All the logs have been cut and the float logs shaped with some u-shaped slots, which will receive the cross beam logs, and sharp ends on one end of each float log and they are left to dry out for seven days. The women make harnesses for the sixteen iwaglamna šunkawakans that will be used for towing the raft. Most of the preparations are made, before the women prepare the rendering of animal fat. They will create some tallow from the rendered animal fat, which they have boiled down in cooking pots giving the logs more time to dry out and lighten, losing their moisture weight.

Much hunting and fishing have supplied meat and fish which is smoked and dried. Water supplies will come from the river and if need be, fresh water mountain streams. A few walega miniyaye (a water jug – Lakota dialect), have been made from freshly killed game and will be filled to use in the future. The next and final task before the raft can be bound together is to grease the logs with the fatty oils and tallow, to seal them and keep them from soaking in water. This is done by the braves and women alike; after this has been completed the logs are rotated in the sun for two more days before the assembling process begins in earnest.

Wanagiyata makes sure the logs are placed according to his drawing and bound with strong tie downs of animal hide ropes and once that has all been done, a pole tenting frame is built on the raft large enough to sleep the entire crew under and be able to cook if needed, on flat stones placed near the door opening. There is room on the outside to move all around the structure, for poling and tending lines from the horses towing from shore.

When all the raft is completed, the 'Story Tellers' stand back and admire their work and are very pleased, as is Wanagiyata.

Oyaka asks Wanagiyata, "This log raft is very heavy, how will we move it into the water without breaking it apart"? Sun Man speaks up, "I will show all with eyes to see."

He picks up one end of the raft and then walks under it, then lifts it up and walks into the river, lowers it and swims out from under the raft, pulls the bow (front) line of the raft to shore, where he ties it off to a large rock. He then pulls the stern (rear of a vessel) line of the raft in close to shore. Then he asks for some help to hold the line, until he can cut a small tree down. He chops a tree and makes two short stakes, sharpened at one end. He then comes back and drives one into the shore by the bow line and reties it to the stake and then he does the same thing at the aft (the stern or rear end of a vessel) of the raft and ties it securely. Everyone jumps up and down laughing and celebrating this incredible act of strength. Sun Man smiles broadly and runs away fast to dry off.

A great night's celebration is in order, Kimimila cooks a fine meal and Wachiwi dances one dance to the delight of all, then Wanagiyata tells them, that he will be on lookout on the bow, when under way, aboard the raft along with Okolaya, while Oyaka tends the lines to the towing horses. The powerful Sun Man will be at the tiller (steering pole) and will steer the raft as Wanagiyata calls out orders as needed, as Captain in charge. After all has been said by the Captain, the great waowešica (a bear in general) comes into camp and yawns and lays down by the fire, Mato Hota has spoken in his silent way, (time to climb into warm blankets), for tomorrow the great adventure upriver begins.

Everyone is up early, but not as early as Kimimila, who brings all to life, with her cooking, when each wake to the

163

odorous aroma coming from her campfire cooking pot. Everyone eats, while Kimimila cleans up and packs her cooking items, and everything is loaded aboard the raft. Sun Man and Wanagiyata harness all the tow horses and tie their riding horses behind the last towing horse; each extra horse is tied with a leadline to one another. It is a long line of horses and they are being led by Mato Hota Brother, with Šungmanitu Ruler on point with both Akita One and Akita Two, ranging out to the right and north side of the horse column. It is a sight to see and soon some will be blessed in this way.

Captain Wanagiyata orders lines to be cast off by Oyaka and Okolaya, first the aft line by Okolaya, then the bow line by Oyaka. The raft starts to move slowly backward until the slack is taken up by the tow lines, then the towing horses begin to walk forward, slowly pulling the raft up river. It is a great start to their river trip west. It is a beautiful day, with a light breeze blowing in their faces as they move up river.

They are making about two miles distance every hour and after five hours, they pull into shore, tie off the raft and tend the animals with water and some dry grasses they have gathered and packed on their riding horses for use, during the day. Nightly they are tethered in grassy areas to feed and rest, as camp is made on shore. If storms come, everyone sleeps on board, and the horses are tethered and hobbled (tie or strap together legs of a horse, or other animal to prevent it from straying).

They have traveled for two days and everything has gone well, there have been some areas, where the raft needed to be tied up, and the horses moved around some trees or boulders, which were close to the water's edge and in the way. When this would happen, the horses were moved around and up stream, and the mighty Sun Man would pull the raft up and around the obstacles and reattach the towlines to the šunkawakans. What a blessing to have this mighty warrior as a 'Story Teller' and part of this mission.

The mission members would usually travel five hours in the morning and three hours in the afternoon giving them around sixteen to seventeen miles of travel per day. They were making good time and were hoping to meet up with some tribes living near the Great River. They have been traveling around a sharp curve winding to the right near the north shore on the fifth day of travel, when Šungmanitu Ruler returns running back to report the presence of a village ahead. Wanagiyata told him and his scouts, along with Mato Hota Brother to join the rear of the column and he would lead the tow-horses forward until, he could make contact with an outer village guard.

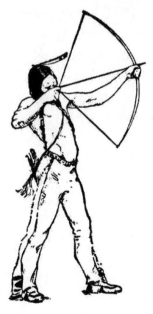

Little do they know, that they were spotted some time ago and many braves are waiting outside the village for them to get in range to be surrounded and confronted with bows drawn with arrows ready to let fly and spears ready to be thrown. No small group could fight against this, if all these weapons are brought to bear and unleashed on a single signal by their Coast Salish Flathead Chief Buffalo Finder.

Nearing the Coast Salish Flathead village, Wanagiyata has a strange feeling come upon his spirit and continues to look for any outside village guard and is surprised he has not been challenged, as he closes in on the village. The mission members all arrive in front of the village, which appears to be abandoned. Wanagiyata calls for Šungmanitu Ruler to come up to his position and asked him to be careful and scout the village for signs of life.

Šungmanitu Ruler starts to move into the village and has moved about ten steps, when two hundred and eighty Coast Salish Flathead warriors come in and block all movement by Wanagiyata and his 'Story Tellers'. They are surrounded, with a multitude of arrows and spears pointed at them. Chief Buffalo Finder is ready to give the signal to attack ekicipa (to meet and attack – Lakota dialect), but holds his signal, when he sees the sight of three wolves and not far behind a huge grizzly bear.

Suddenly, all the skies turn almost dark and lightning bursts across the sky from west to east in rapid succession. All witnessing this are frozen in fear, except the members of the 'Story Tellers', although their horses are startled, but do not try to bolt off from their harnesses. Soon a blue and white tunnel of light forms from the west and moves across the darkened sky in between the lightning strikes, Chief Buffalo Finder's hand is raised and all the Coast Salish Flathead warriors are afraid and look back and forth to the sky and their chief, confused and afraid, not knowing what to do.

Until we join our 'Story Tellers' surrounded and being held in danger by the Coast Salish Flathead warriors and Chief Buffalo Finder, our next Campfire Story Telling – "We Come In Peace, We Are 'Story Tellers'." May Wakantanka guide you and keep you safe.

Chapter 9

We Come In Peace, We Are 'Story Tellers'

The mission of 'Story Tellers' has arrived at the Coast Salish Flathead Indian village in the northwestern wilderness. Only to be surprised by one hundred and eighty Coast Salish Flathead warriors, with bows drawn and spears ready to be unleashed on them. Chief Buffalo Finder is ready to give the signal to attack our Oglala Lakota Indians and one mighty Crow. A darkened sky filled with lightning flashes traveling west to east in rapid succession appears. All seeing this phenomenon are held in fear and remain still, except for the 'Story Tellers' and their animal Scouts, Šungmanitu (a wolf) Aitancan (a ruler over), and his two faithful scout brothers, Akita (to seek or hunt for, as something lost) One and Akita Two from his wolf pack —in modern day South Dakota— near the Oglala Lakota village, where most of the 'Story Tellers' live. Another very strong and ferocious member of the mission is Mato Hota (a grizzly bear) Titakuye (immediate relatives), a giant grizzly bear brother to the 'Story Tellers'.

The sight of seeing three šungmanitus and a mato hota, friendly to the strange Indians who have come on a large raft, being drawn by many šunkawakans (a horse), which Chief Buffalo Finder has never seen, also, by anyone in his village. Seeing this has stayed (to hold back, detain, or restrain, as from going further) Chief Buffalo Finder's hand signal to launch an attack.

The lightning is still streaking across the sky and soon a blue and white tunnel of light forms in the western sky and moves across the darkened sky in between the lightning bolts and begins to move toward the Coast Salish Flathead village. Chief Buffalo Finder has his hand held high in the air to signal an attack, and he has not moved it. The tunnel of blue and white light comes down between the 'Story Tellers' and Chief Buffalo Finder and Tatanka Ska Son (Son of Wakantanka) appears from the tunnel of light and it disappears instantly.

Chief Buffalo Finder slowly kneels before Tatanka Ska Son, as do all his warriors. Tatanka Ska Son speaks in His low Voice,

"Lower your hand, held high in the hatred of the unknown, I and My messengers, the 'Story Tellers' come in peace. Warriors put down your wicat'es (an instrument with which to kill with) and welcome My 'Story Tellers', who have come to tell you of My Father, Wakantanka (God), and Me, His only Son. Bring Me all the sick and those who are suffering and place them here before Me. All rise up on your feet and be not afraid. Go now and bring Me your sick and suffering."

Chief Buffalo Finder instructs every Coast Salish Flathead warrior to run and bring all sick and suffering, as Tatanka Ska Son has asked. Soon many come and sit or lay in between Chief Buffalo Finder and Tatanka Ska Son. New words are spoken by Tatanka Ska Son, "Please come forward Wanagiyata (in the land of spirits), and bring your animal brothers, that the Coast Salish Flathead people may see that they come in peace and know that I love them. Wanagiyata, I am going to leave now and return to My Father's loving side. Touch My side and feel your healing powers flow through you, that you may heal these who have come before Me."

Wanagiyata walks forward with his faithful animal scouts and brothers, and touches the side of Tatanka Ska Son, and feels His power flow through him. Tatanka Ska Son slowly lifts off into the western sky and soon is out of sight to all left in awe among the Coast Salish Flathead Indian tribe.

"Great chief, I am Wanagiyata of the Oglala Lakota and these are my friends and wives. Among them is a mighty warrior of the Crow Nation, Sun (Axxaashe – Crow dialect) Man (Bachhee – Crow dialect), who you will get to know soon. What is your name?" Chief Buffalo Finder is surprised that Wanagiyata speaks his dialect, but is pleased he does and

169

answers, "I am called Buffalo Finder, chief of this Coast Salish Flathead village." Wanagiyata goes to the first sick person he is nearest too, and touches her forehead. She has been crippled by a bear attack when she was only five years old, before her father and uncle shot arrows into the bear and he was wounded and turned on them and wounded them before he died. Next, Wanagiyata goes around and touches each of the sick and suffering, which number over twenty, some are old and have no teeth with which to chew and they are thin and unhealthy. "Rise up all before me that I have touched, you are healed, your health returned to you by Wakantanka, rejoice in His love," says Wanagiyata.

When those who were sick and suffering stand up slowly and look around and see that all have been healed, they start to rejoice and chant. Now all the Coast Salish Flathead villagers and warriors, gather around the 'Story Tellers' and welcome them. The village is alive with activity. Wanagiyata is shown a place to pitch his tipis (teepee or tent or lodge) and make camp.

He is invited to a celebration to be held in their honor and a great feast of buffalo and other meat dishes will be served, along with fish, fresh from the river they have nearby, as a great breadbasket most of the year.

Once camp has been setup and the horses cared for and tethered (tie an animal with rope or chain so as to restrict its movement) and guarded, always by one of the animal scouts, usually Akita One, who loves the horses he guards, as if they were his own children. He likes to hear their noises of whinny and coughing and he knows they are alright and not under stress, it makes him happy and he is glad to guard them.

Chief Buffalo Finder has invited Wanagiyata to his tipi to

smoke the pipe of friendship and he is glad to be there among new friends. Chief Buffalo Finder explains how he got his name to Wanagiyata, saying that when he was a young boy his name was Little Toad, and he was out hunting for deer, as meat was short in supply for his family and village. Instead of finding deer, he ran into a small herd of buffalo standing in a clearing in the forest. He ran as fast as he could back to get his father, One Wolf, who brought other braves to hunt them. The hunt was a big success and his tribe needed the buffalo meat, as their supply of buffalo meat was completely gone. Little Toad was renamed from that day, Buffalo Finder and was revered among his people for saving them from hunger, and now he is chief among them.

The chief asked Wanagiyata what his name meant and how he got it. This story was amazing to hear and Chief Buffalo Finder is humbled by it, and now he has belief in Wakantanka and Tatanka Ska Son. He is overjoyed, when he is told by Wanagiyata, that because he believes in Them, he will live forever with Them in Mahpiya (Heaven) and among all the animals gone before from this Earth. The story of the 'Earlier Earth' was spellbinding to him and that is just part of what the chief wants his people to hear from the 'Story Tellers' while they are here.

Soon sounds of drums and singing are heard and Wanagiyata goes to his small camp and invites his wife, Wachiwi (dancing girl), Crow Sun Man, Oyaka (to tell, report, relate) and his wife, Gidagaakoons (fawn – Chippewa dialect), and Okolaya (to have as a friend), along with his wife, Kimimila (butterfly), to join him by Chief Buffalo Finder's tipi for food and entertainment in a Coast Salish Flathead way. Akita One is staying with the horses and will be relieved for a short time by Akita Two, so he can join and eat along with all the celebrants on this special night along with new friends of the Coast Salish Flathead people.

When the 'Story Tellers' arrive at Chief Buffalo Finders tipi, his wife Running Waters is feeding the giant mato hota the full back leg of a tatanka (a male buffalo), which he is enjoying greatly, as he chews this huge buffalo leg with no ha (skin or hide with hair), held between his great paws, occasionally h'eh'eya (slobbering – Lakota dialect), which makes them all laugh in fun. She has served him the meat, just as he likes it best, raw and juicy. Many children are seated around him watching him eat and glad it is not one of them.

One of the children seated next to Mato Hota Brother is a little girl that is now grown, who was mauled by a grizzly bear. Now she is healed and unafraid of this giant waowešica (a bear in general) among bears, the great grizzly of the north, who fears no living thing he encounters. Wanagiyata looks around and sees Šungmanitu Ruler and Akita Two with many young Coast Salish Flathead Indian boys, who are feeding them meat and petting them lovingly, as new best friends. There is a bond between animals and human beings, when no fear or bad intentions are held between them, as Wakantanka intended it to be so. It is that way in Mahpiya this very day and always, forever more.

After everyone has eaten and performed dances and songs, Chief Buffalo Finder, can wait no more in his excitement to have his Coast Salish Flathead people know the story of the 'Earlier Earth' and this Mother Earth and how it came to be. He stands and a single drum beat is sounded and all goes quiet. "My people, we have seen miracles and sights never seen before in our lands. Many have been healed and made as before, by Wanagiyata, through the Power of Wakantanka, to whom we bow down. Wanagiyata will tell his greatest story of two Earths, as I will it be so," says Chief Buffalo Finder. He pulls Wanagiyata to his feet and sits down to listen once again to this greatest of stories he has ever heard.

Wanagiyata tells the story of the 'Earlier Earth' God created, before Mother Earth, in "The Chosen Ones Oglala Warriors," which takes all those listening, to believe in what his story telling has unfolded to them. They are joyful in the knowledge that they can be 'saved', by simply believing in Wakantanka and His Son, Tatanka Ska Son. All they need to do is ask for forgiveness, from Wakantanka for any wrong doings they have done in their past, and have sorrow for those wrong doings.

How simple it is to be 'saved' and how wonderful to know you will live forever in 'Mahpiya' with them along with all creatures gone before. Many will not sleep this night, as excitement grips them with thoughts of how fortunate they all are, that the 'Story Tellers' have come to teach them of many wondrous happenings that they have experienced and will share during their visit in their Coast Salish Flathead village.

Morning, finds Kimimila cooking a fine early meal of hehaka (the male elk) meat in a stew with beans and peas. Sun Man is checking on his horse and all the others as well, which he is very faithful in his duties to Wakantanka's gift to him, along with his great strength. Soon the Coast Salish Flathead villagers will see him in action. All the šunkawakans cared for, Sun Man returns to their small camp and then he goes with Wanagiyata to meet in private with Chief Buffalo Finder and smoke the pipe. It is a custom he enjoys, because it is a time of 'the talk' and prized among the many tribes, who have tobacco.

A Coast Salish Flathead brave on guard, escorts the two braves to Chief Buffalo Finder's tipi and announces them. They are invited in and are seated around a warm fire, and served hot White Oak tea, —made from the bark of a white oak tree— by his tawicu (his wife), Running Waters, the good chief's very knowledgeable wife in the use of various plants and herbs, she has learned from their village 'medicine man'.

His name is Waašape in Lakota dialect (dirty or soiled hands), which he is called, because he is always digging for roots and herbs and other plants. His name may seem oddly disparaging, however, when one is sick, they always go to see him, if they have something to trade for his treatment, that is how he lives and maintains respect among his tribal members, just as most 'medicine men' do in other tribes.

Chief Buffalo Finder lights a pipe of tobacco and puffs on it to get it started and then passes it to Wanagiyata, who takes a puff and nods in approval and passes it to Sun Man, who takes a long puff, exhales the smoke and smiles, nodding his head in approval, and then passes it back to the Coast Salish Flathead chief. Now that the formalities have been completed, Wanagiyata is asked about the story of how he met Sun Man by Chief Buffalo Finder.

He relates the story about how he came to know his Crow friend. The story Wanagiyata told was how he and his Oglala Lakota brothers came upon him as a captive of the Jicarilla Apache (see appendix page 214) and was being tortured by them. He told of the rescue and how they became friends when he was named Arikara (running wolf – Crow dialect) and Wanagiyata was called Okiziwakiya (to cause to heal up).

During the story telling, he was not told how Arikara became Sun Man and maybe someday chief of his Crow village. That would come, but, it would not be told in words this day. Chief

Buffalo Finder invites his guest to go on a big buffalo hunt with six of his braves, on the next days early light. They accept this invitation most graciously. Later that night it would be the Oglala Lakota who would be performing for the Coast Salish Flathead villagers.

Wanagiyata has asked Wachiwi to dance the many dances she knows, to honor these oyate (a people, nation, tribe or band) and new friends. She has agreed to do so, if he will tell a story of how they came to be married to introduce her before she performs. Also, Oyaka and Okolaya would do the drumming. After Wachiwi finishes her dancing, Kimimila is to sing songs she has made about butterflies and who follow a small deer through his life and show him how to find food he likes best.

Last, but not least, to sing, in her Chippewa dialect is Gidagaakoons, who will dance two dances she loves to do and sing one song about her people. This will conclude their performances for this night, but more is coming as they live among the Coast Salish Flathead for as long as they feel they can help them and learn about their customs.

The next morning, a hunt is taken by Wanagiyata, Oyaka, Okolaya, and Sun Man, when they appear at Chief Buffalo Finder's tipi, each one leading two horses, except Wanagiyata, who has one horse following him on a leadline. This is a big surprise to the chief and his braves. Wanagiyata tells them to mount the iwaglamnas (an extra or fresh horse). They are very happy to have this chance to see these fine horses close up, let alone to be given the opportunity to ride on one. Everyone is mounted and the experienced horseman will lead the spare horses with the Coast Salish Flathead braves and their chief being carried along on their backs, which are covered with tatanka blankets.

Wanagiyata whistles loudly and Šungmanitu Ruler and Akita Two run to join in the hunt. Akita One is left to guard the remaining horses and he is glad to do it. Not to be left behind, Mato Ḣota Brother lumbers in to be a part of this hunt, which he really enjoys. Some of the Coast Salish Flathead boys have been hanging around Sun Man and have learned to feed and water the horses, and will do so, under the eagle eyes of the wives, who will make sure they do a good job.

Chief Buffalo Finder, directs Wanagiyata on the way to go, and is enjoying riding instead of walking at a brisk pace. The animal scouts are walking beside the leader, Wanagiyata, and his horse. The hunt is on its second day, when Wanagiyata asked if Chief Buffalo Finder would like a little help in finding the buffalo. Wanagiyata was glad to see what he could do to make it a faster hunt, so he sent out Šungmanitu Ruler and his two šungmanitu scouts, his brother wolves, Akita Two, who went out left and Akita One to the right leading the hunt.

It is early afternoon, when Šungmanitu Ruler runs back fast from scouting and tells Wanagiyata that he has spotted a large herd of tatanka about a mile away. The hunters continue forward, but halt and sneak in crawling over the top of a small rise in the ground.

The horses have been tethered and all hunters are peering over the rise, looking at the main buffalo herd grazing quietly about two hundred yards away. Sun Man, whispers to Wanagiyata and then Chief Buffalo Finder that he is going to hunt the bulls, that are fighting and that they should wait to launch their hunt on the main herd when he signals them.

176

He will signal when he is close enough to the fighting pair of big bull tatankas. Wanagiyata will let Chief Buffalo Finder and his hunters rush in on foot to take as many as they can, before he and his Oglala Lakota brothers ride in and chase the running herd and drop some with arrows and spears.

All eyes are on Sun Man, who puts on a buffalo hide with heavy fur on it, and quietly walks around the main herd and then, he moves in faster on the fighting bulls, who do not see him or care, for to them, he appears like a very small buffalo calf chasing around. As he closes in on them, he speeds up and rams them, knocking both over, rolling them down and then he hits one in the head behind his great horns with only his fist, killing him instantly.

The other bull regains his feet and thunders off away from the main herd. Sun Man catches him and grabs his rear legs, lifts him off his feet and then slams him in the chest by his heart with his fist and he is dead without suffering any pain. He pulls the second kill over to the first kill and waits for the others to start their hunt, upon seeing his signal.

They are still looking at what the great and powerful Sun

Man has just done, and are totally in shock, not believing what their own eyes have witnessed. Wanagiyata has mounted his horse and is ready to go on the hunt, but will wait for Chief Buffalo Finder to make his hunting move on foot with his braves. Finally, seeing that it is time for them to move in fast on foot and shoot arrows and throw spears at those they pick out in the main herd to hunt, Chief Buffalo Finder, scores a big bull, with his bow and arrow and three of his braves each get one.

The other three Coast Salish Flathead braves do not hit their killing mark with their spears and only wound them. They all ran away some distance and then one wounded big bull turns around and charges at one of the hunters and is about to gore him in the back as he tried to run to his right side.

The big bull just missed his mark with his long curved sharp left horn. The bull swings around and finds Sun Man standing in front of the fearful Coast Salish Flathead hunter who wounded him. Mad and in pain, the buffalo bull charges the powerful warrior and when he lowers his head to strike, Sun Man steps to the side and comes down with a hatchet chopping blow with the side of his powerful palm hand. He breaks the big buffalo bull's neck, like a twig, although the sound is the sound like the crack of lightning hitting a tree.

All the Coast Salish Flathead are watching the power of Sun Man, when Wanagiyata, Oyaka, and Okolaya gallop by them in pursuit of the main herd now in full flight. The Oglala Lakota brothers, Wanagiyata with his spear, Oyaka with a well-placed arrow, and Okolaya with his trusty spear, have all scored a clean kill.

This hunt has been an incredible hunt, and one which will be passed on by the Coast Salish Flathead hunters. Many campfires with 'Story Tellers' will pass on the story of the great hunt and what the great and powerful Sun Man did. All the buffalos, including the other wounded buffalo, Sun Man hunted down and make a quick kill to end his suffering and he was carried back to the others and field dressed. The tatanka meat is loaded on the šun'onk'onpa (a pony or dog travois – Lakota dialect), even with every horse loaded down; it is good Mato Hota is along on this hunt. Even he is fitted with a travois and all the meat from a total of eleven big buffalo bulls are harvested and the journey back to the Coast Salish Flathead village is longer than finding the buffalo herd hunting ground.

Two days pass when the hunters return, all are exhausted, with the exception of Sun Man, most especially the šunkawakans who have pulled heavy loads of tatanka meat for many miles. The precious meat, so important to survival, is turned over to the women of the Coast Salish Flathead village, to process into jerky and smoked meat for at least a two-month supply, to feed their large village.

The horses are given a bath with warm water and some pine bark mixed in for freshness, and then they are watered and fed some dried grass and corn. The hunters head for their tipis, food and their blankets for much needed rest. The celebration for the hunt will wait until tomorrow. Sun Man, stayed out by the horses in his tipi, as he always does, with the company of Akita One, who keeps guard near his horse, with one eye open.

The next day the village is actively preparing to celebrate the hunt in the early evening, there is much talking and whispering going on among the villagers. Word of the incredible strength of Sun Man has spread throughout the village. When Sun Man walks among the villagers the next day; everyone treats him with even more respect, than he had before.

He decides to walk into the woods nearby and stops to lean on a rock and watch the river and water fowl taking off and landing on the water, and is reminded of his flight on Tatanka Ska Son's back high in the mountains. His thoughts are interrupted by a scream coming from upstream along his side of the river. He jumps into action and runs as fast as he can over rocks and boulders toward the now repeated screams.

A Coast Salish Flathead maiden is being mauled by a huge golden colored grizzly, while washing horse hair blankets in the river. Sun Man jumps on the great bear's back, pulls his massive head back, grabs his jaws and spreads them far apart, breaking them and then, he snaps his neck breaking it like a small twig one would step on while walking. The young maiden, is mortally wounded by the waowešica (a bear in general) attack, her right arm has been torn off and she has bite marks on her neck and face. Her scalp is bleeding badly and torn half off from the blow of the grizzly's his huge paw, with long claws as ripping weapons.

It is a terrible mauling and she has also, been clawed by the bear's long sharp claws in her stomach. She looks up seeing Sun Man's face and passes out. Sun Man scoops her up, grabs her severed right arm and runs at full speed to the tipi of Wanagiyata, passing by Chief Buffalo Finder, who sees his daughter in Sun Man's arms and covered with blood.

Chief Buffalo Finder follows Sun Man, as fast as he can run. Sun Man yells for help as he enters Wanagiyata tipi with Chief Buffalo Finder close behind him. The strong hands of Sun Man, gently lays the wounded maiden down on a blanket and places her right arm, which has been torn off, on her chest. Chief

Buffalo Finder is in a complete panic.

Wanagiyata prays over her, while placing her arm back close to her shoulder and soon, it moves back in place, and each wound begins to heal up right before Chief Buffalo Finders wet eyes. The maiden stirs and wakes to consciousness and is in no pain, but screams, remembering being attacked by the giant golden bear. Sun Man leans in close to her face and says, "Fear not, you are safe now and healed by Wanagiyata." She remembers his face, as the last thing she saw, before passing out with the thought she was dying. She stops screaming and realizes, she is safe, as her father, rubs her head lovingly.

Chief Buffalo Finder and his wife Running Waters are with their daughter Blossom Flowers in their tipi, celebrating her being saved by Sun Man and healed by Wanagiyata. Blossom Flowers, realizes all that has happened to her and knows that her believing in Wakantanka and Tatanka Ska Son, is the reason she has been saved and healed of terrible wounds. She has been praying, as have her father and mother, giving all thanks and praise to Wakantanka, for sending Wanagiyata and Sun Man to their village.

Sun Man's face is embedded in the mind of Blossom Flowers, and now moving into her heart. Blossom Flowers face is beautiful, and she is tall and slim and when she walks, she walks with grace and carries herself as a chief's daughter with dignity, not to ever disgrace him or her family.

Everyone has gathered for the celebration of the hunt, waiting on Chief Buffalo Finder to start the celebration, with opening words. He steps out of his tipi leading by their hands both, his wife, Running Waters, and daughter, Blossom Flowers. A great cheer erupts from all the villagers and chanting and singing erupts, many begin to jump up and down in happiness, all because of the saving of Blossom Flowers by Sun Man and the healing by Wanagiyata. This celebration goes on for about five minutes, as the chief and his family smile looking around at everyone.

Finally, Chief Buffalo Finder raises his hands calling for silence. All goes quiet and the chief, calls for Wanagiyata and Sun Man to join him. When they do, he steps between them and grabs their wrist and raises their arms high. The villagers begin cheering loudly in approval, showing great joy.

When the cheering dies down, the chief begins to speak, "My people know that these two great men saved my daughter Blossom Flowers, from the hungry bear's jaws and the terrible wounds of sure death. I believe in Wakantanka and His Son, Tatanka Ska Son, who sent them to our village, to teach us of His love. I am most thankful for His gift of life, my heart is full."

The celebration begins and Wanagiyata is seated by Chief Buffalo Finder on one side, and his wife, Wachiwi, on the other side. Sun Man is seated by the other side of the chief, next to his wife, Running Waters. Blossom Flowers, is on her feet and brings food to Wanagiyata and then she serves Sun Man his food, honoring both men in her own way.

Sun Man saw more than thankfulness in the beautiful eyes of Blossom Flowers than merely thanks, he saw into her heart and was deeply touched by her warmth. This moment, is fixed in his mind, and he cannot move it aside with other thoughts of his tribe or friends back in his village, even many admiring Crow maidens.

After the big celebration has ended, he spends a long

sleepless night with the horses, which normally fill him with comfort, but not this night, for he is truly lonely for the very first time. He is puzzled by this feeling, and starts to pray about this confusion to Wakantanka for answers. The answer to his prayers would come soon to this most powerful of men to ever live on Mother Earth.

The next night, finds Sun Man suffering deep loneness, even more than previously on other days. He is able to speak to anyone after being gifted the ability to speak all languages and dialects by Wakantanka. This gift came to him in the battle on the high cliff edge with the Jicarilla Apache. Still, he cannot rid himself of this loneness, no matter how many he may speak with.

He has been staying to himself and others have noticed. Kimimila, who is the closest of the wives to him, has noticed, he has been spending more time with the horses and less with his closest friends. She has seen how Sun Man watches Blossom Flowers, whenever he sees her walking by or sees them near one another. She knows from this, he is troubled.

Kimimila takes food to Sun Man, as he has not come from his tipi near the horses for early or noon meals and she is worried about him. She asks Wanagiyata, before she goes, if he knows what is troubling their friend, he answers no, and that she should go and serve him food and see if he is well.

Kimimila arrives in front of Sun Man's tipi with a basket of food and announces herself and is invited in. Sun Man is first to speak, "Kimimila, my sister, you are most welcome in my tipi at all times in friendship! Thank you for coming, your food smell is a good sign, my nose is working." "My brother, it is good to see you, you are missed among us. What troubles you, are you unwell"? asked Kimimila.

"I do not know what steals my will to be myself, my joy has left me. I pray for words of wisdom from Wakantanka," answers Sun Man as he continues after a pause, "I feel alone, even when around my šunkawakan and friends." Kimimila asks, "May I speak words from my heart in friendship, as I feel they have directed me to your side"?

"Please speak your heart, I will value your words, as I value you," he answers. Kimimila says, "I believe you are lonely for the companionship and love of a good wife. I have seen the way you and Blossom Flowers look at each other and I see love dwells among you both. I have grown to know Blossom Flowers and I believe she has a good heart and it is beautiful, like her ways. Go to her my brother and speak of your feelings for her, do not let this light in your heart go dim, for it may never light up, as a campfire of warmth again. That is all I have to say my brother, forgive me if my words are not welcomed, I have spoken them from my heart." She leaves him to think about her words.

Sun Man, realizes, that Kimimila has been sent with a message from Wakantanka in answer to his prayers and a great joy passes into his heart, as he realizes, that he is lonely because he is in love with Blossom Flowers, who has been on his mind constantly. He decides to go to her father and ask if he may court her, only if she and her mother, also agree. He eats hurriedly and then, he goes to asks Chief Buffalo Finder to walk with him and as they walk, he explains his feelings to him during their long walk together by the wide river. Chief Buffalo Finder does not show any feelings on his face about this request, but says his answer will come at morning sun.

Sun Man can hardly sleep, thinking about what answer he

will receive from Chief Buffalo Finder in the morning. It is very early in the morning and Sun Man is standing in front of Chief Buffalo Finder's tipi, waiting for long minutes, before he announces himself. The flap of the tipi opens and Chief Buffalo Finder emerges with Blossom Flowers' soft hand in his rough big hand. "It is good you are here early! My wife and my daughter have been talking and giggling all night and I am going to find fish by the waters of peace. Here, (giving Blossom Flowers' hand over to Sun Man) take my daughter for a walk by the river, or I will have no sleep again this night," says the chief, heading off west toward the river.

Sun Man is over joyed to be holding her hand as they walk along the river, but is quiet. Blossom Flowers speaks up softly. "Sun Man, you honor me, by asking to see me and now that you do, what words will you speak? Before you speak, I must tell you that you have dwelled in my mind and I hold you in my heart, all this since the day you saved me. I do not have feelings for you for that reason alone, my feelings have life, because I feel you have feelings for me in your heart, for I have seen it in your eyes. I hope I am not blind or being without reasoning powers."

Sun Man speaks in answer to her words, "Your reasoning powers are strong and tell a story true, I am lonely for you, because I am not by your side. I love you and have suffered, not being near you. I will ask for your hand in marriage, if you want to be my wife and give me children in this life"?

The two love struck pair, look deeply into each other's eyes and hug one another tightly and laugh joyfully. Sun Man picks up Blossom Flowers and runs at full speed back through the woods with her safely in his powerful arms, as she screams in surprise and happiness. Her father, up river, hears her and smiles broadly.

A week has passed and many days the 'Story Tellers' have been visiting and teaching all the Coast Salish Flathead villagers about Wakantanka and His Son, and the many experiences they have had, since Tatanka Ska Son came into their lives and saved them so many times. After the 'Story Tellers' have been around many campfires visiting, some new 'Story Tellers' are being made here in this large Coast Salish Flathead village. There is also, other important activities taking place in the tipi of Running Waters, as she is making a special taha (a deerskin) dress for her daughter's wedding soon to come. The visiting 'Story Tellers' wives have been preparing for the wedding also, crafting many gifts, during this time of anticipation.

Sun Man, has been given a horse by Wanagiyata for a wedding gift, to give to Chief Buffalo Finder. He has only asked for the gift of a good pipe, for his daughter's hand, as he is not greedy and is honored to have the most powerful son-in-law that has ever lived. He will be honored to have Sun Man as a member of his family and give him grandchildren. Maybe even a very powerful grandson, who could be chief when he no longer walks Mother Earth. Sun Man has given Chief Buffalo Finder this great gift before the wedding and he is very happy to have it. He is taking daily lessons from Sun Man on riding and caring for this wonderful gift. The two have bonded, as father and son. It is as it should be, a good thing.

In the meantime, word has come that The Nez Perce Indians are on a raiding mission and have chosen to come against their old enemy, the Coast Salish Flathead people. All the village is on a war footing and Chief Buffalo Finder calls his 'Elders' to counsel him and he invites his powerful new friends the 'Story Tellers' to attend. The chief asked for advice from all present and states he has been in prayer to Wakantanka to give him a plan for war.

Wanagiyata asks the chief if he may speak and is granted this request without hesitation, even though he is not a tribal member. Wanagiyata, speaks up, "My friends, it has been my experience, when threatened by a war coming to my village; I have taken the takpe (to come upon, attack) to the enemy before on the battle ground of my choosing. Why risk your village or people, when we could find a good defensive place to meet the Nez Perce and surprise them with a good battle plan. We will go to fight with your Coast Salish Flathead warriors, if you wish it to be so. Those are my words, my friends."

The council discussed what Wanagiyata had told them after the 'Story Tellers' leave. The Elders have listened to their words of council and have agreed it was a 'good plan' and they would like their help. They believed Wakantanka was with them and would be with those who fought by their side. It is zuya (war).

Chief Buffalo Finder is leading over two hundred well prepared warriors, including his new friends, the 'Story Tellers', on his new horse. Those on foot are loaded with weapons for a great battle and Sun Man rides his horse beside him, with Wanagiyata riding behind him with his brothers, including his animal brothers, who are out front scouting the way forward.

We will follow them into battle soon, in our next Campfire Story Telling – "A Great Battle With The Nez Perce Raiders." Be safe, until then and may Wakantanka be with you.

Oglala Lakota Chief Flying Hawk

Chief Flying Hawk (Oglala Lakota: Čhetáŋ Kiŋyáŋ in Standard Lakota Orthography; also known as Moses Flying Hawk; March 1854 – December 24, 1931) was an Oglala Lakota warrior, historian, educator and philosopher. Flying Hawk's life chronicles the history of the Oglala Lakota people through the 19th and early 20th centuries, as he fought to deflect the worst effects of white rule; educate his people and preserve sacred Oglala Lakota land and heritage.-Wikipedia

Chapter 10

A Great Battle With The Nez Perce Raiders

The sun is high and our mixed band of Indian warriors lead by Chief Buffalo Finder of the Coast Salish Flathead Indians, accompanied by two hundred Coast Salish Flathead braves and all the visiting 'Story Tellers', including the animal scouts and friends. Šungmanitu (a wolf) Aitancan (the ruler over) the fast and wise one —referred to, as Šungmanitu Ruler— and his two šungmanitu scouts Akita (to seek or hunt for, as something lost) One and Akita Two, along with the huge and powerful fearless Mato Ḣota (a grizzly bear) Titakuye (the immediate relatives)

—referred to, as Mato Ḣota Brother—.

This is a force to fear, but the mighty Nez Perce, do not know of them or their strength. They also, do not know they have been seen, by others and Chief Buffalo Finder has been warned by a friendly tribe near them. This friendly tribe has seen Nez Perce prepare for a vengeful war. Many years of hatred has been carried in the hearts of those who are taught in their young years to hate from stories of olden times told by their forefathers, who fought many wars and made many raids against other tribes.

The wound is open and never closes because, with years of hate taught to the young ones, it never dies or scabs over. Until a new understanding can take place through an act of mercy or other gifts of the heart are given, there will be no peace. It is a challenge to heal the hatred created by a long line of hatemongers, who in most cases have had no physical knowledge or experience in what they teach to their young.

This hatred has been passed down from many campfires, from long ago. Now, it has reared its ugly head and is set in motion, by a young and ambitious Nez Perce brave, who has taken over from his father, Chief Walks Alone, who was a powerful chief, and held peaceful ways until he died.

Now his son is chief, and wants to establish his power, and show his ability as a great warrior, to earn the respect of his people and he has decided to wage war against the old enemy of the Nez Perce to the east, the Coast Salish Flathead people. Now the new Chief Walking Winds is leading a powerful raiding party of over six hundred Nez Perce braves.

Šungmanitu Ruler and Akita One and Akita Two are out front scouting and have come to a narrow area of a mountain pass, Šungmanitu Ruler turns back and reports his scouting knowledge to Wanagiyata (in the land of spirits), who shares it with Chief Buffalo Finder and they are eager to see the area and move their horses forward ahead of the main body of Coast Salish Flathead braves. When they reach this area, they know the Nez Perce will have to come through this area to approach their village.

Chief Buffalo Finder heeds the advice of Wanagiyata, who believes, this would be a good place to ambush the Nez Perce, in a surprise attack. They do not know the strength in numbers of the Nez Perce, and must take any advantage of a battle area, they can find. This area looks like it will be very good to defend. The pass narrows down to the length of two horses head to tail in one area. It is surrounded by big boulders, which would be difficult to climb over, without attracting many arrows during the attempted climb, by those who control this narrow pass.

All preparations are put in place, before the main Coast Salish Flathead war party arrives. All warriors are placed in positions of advantage, and are completely out of sight to any force approaching from the west. A cold camp is made a short distance from all assigned positions. And scouts are placed for security and to insure, they are not surprised by the enemy. Wanagiyata has sent Šungmanitu Ruler and his loyal šungmanitu scouts out three miles from the pass, to watch for the enemy Nez Perce. All preparations for battle have been set in place in two days. It will be a waiting game for the Coast Salish Flathead and their 'Story Teller' friends, who will fight beside them in the coming battle.

Chief Buffalo Finder, Wanagiyata and Sun Man (of the Crow tribe) have given instructions to their Coast Salish Flathead warriors, to make more arrows and spears and tomahawks, while waiting for the upcoming battle. Sun Man has made some great battle plans and is sharing them. He has asked that fifty warriors go back to a river they crossed the day before arriving at the pass and collect river rocks that they can hold in their hands and wrap their fingers half way around. Each brave is to collect at least fifty rounded river rocks and bring them to him, in all haste; he has a plan, a surprise attack for the Nez Perce.

Sun Man has scouted the entire area around the pass, he looks at different locations from the position they will hold and the position the Nez Perce will be coming from or defending. He moves some huge boulders, placing them in different areas, making sure he can move to each position as needed. His plan is to be able to move to them and have cover from in-coming arrows or spears, after he throws river rocks at them from many different positions.

He personally gathers some larger rocks and places them around above the pass, along with some big boulders. He is very busy and has amazed everyone with his great strength and stamina. He will sleep, once he has readied his war plans.

Chief Buffalo Finder and Wanagiyata have agreed on a plan Wanagiyata has shared, after scouting the area carefully, so that no signs of them or their warriors show that scouting has been made in the area. They call all warriors together and instruct everyone in where, they will be positioned and how to fight from that assigned location, and be ready to move to other positions, when signals are given from Chief Buffalo Finder or Wanagiyata.

Oyaka (to tell, report, relate) and Okolaya (to have as a friend) have been given twenty warriors each to command and are training them in the battle plans they have been given. They may use their šunkawakans (a horse), but only if needed, the 'Chosen Ones' can't afford the loss of any to the enemy.

Sun Man has assigned two braves to guard his horse back behind the eastern entrance to the pass. He knows his great strength rests in the safety and wellbeing of his horse, given to him by Wakantanka and this gift has conditions, which he understands and follows religiously. He will need his great strength for this battle and is glad to use it to help his friends, the Coast Salish Flathead Indians, in defense of their village, soon to be his people by marriage.

Šungmanitu Ruler and his scout brothers, Akita One and Two, return and report the enemy is steadily advancing, each one is loaded down with many arrows, spears and tomahawks and stone clubs. Most of them are wearing war paint and are chanting in low tones. They are moving in a narrow grouping, which is not widely spaced, showing no fear of discovery, as they believe they have days before they will reach the Coast Salish Flathead village and are not aware of anyone standing in their way.

It will be at least two to three days before the enemy will reach the Coast Salish Flathead army of warriors. All is ready and quiet will be required of everyone, in case the enemy has some forward scouts out leading the attacking Nez Perce forces.

Šungmanitu Ruler further reported that the Nez Perce had four scouts out in front of the enemy's main body, but only by few hundred yards, and were relaying reports back to the young Nez Perce Chief Walking Winds. Their report tells him of the best route to follow, as they moved through the rough terrain for a full days travel on foot. They make a camp, with campfire for cooking each night. Šungmanitu Ruler's report is very detailed and it is welcomed by both Wanagiyata and Chief Buffalo Finder, after Wanagiyata tells him what has been reported.

The first part of the battle plan will be put into action the day before the enemy warriors reach the pass by Chief Buffalo Finder and Wanagiyata. Many arrows and spears have been made and are readied by each Coast Salish Flathead brave in his assigned fighting position. All is ready and tonight will be the last regular camp made before every precaution will be put in place to insure, no discovery of the Coast Salish Flathead can be made by any enemy scouts. No sign of any presence of the Coast Salish Flathead can be found at the western entrance to the pass exist. All efforts to protect the ground conditions there were used, as preparations to defend the pass were made.

Šungmanitu Ruler and his scouts have been out scouting and have returned to report, that the enemy Nez Perce, should be arriving the next day in mid-morning, based on their present rate of travel. Chief Buffalo Finder orders the first part of the battle plan to be activated. Sun Man and Mato Hota Brother, disappear into the night from the cold camp location. The great battle has yet to begin, and only the animals sense foreboding and have lessened their night sounds. However, the šunkmanitus (coyotes) are barking and singing out for a companion to join them in the night, with little interest in what is about to take place between to lethal forces, not affecting them directly.

Meanwhile, the young Nez Perce Chief Walking Winds has broken camp and is heading toward the pass, making good steady progress, with his braves well rested and eager for battle to build their standing with their new chief and have other stories of their bravery in battle to be told by many campfires among the Nez Perce people.

Most warriors are known by their hunting, fishing and fighting skills and these skills are all important to maidens, looking for a good husband and father for her children and that is the main value in men, they look for. However, most marriages are made by sale or trade, and the women have no choice in the matter, except to flirt in small ways to have the brave she likes barter for her, and many braves are unaware this is their way, some marriages are a 'good trade' and love binds the marriage in a true friendship.

This very day, there will be many less braves that will be available for marriage, as well as fewer fathers returning to wives, that is some of the cost of war, more is the loss of a father to his children. Chief Walks Alone knew this and kept his warriors from unnecessary fighting, but now the old chief is gone and new lessons need to be taught.

Chief Walking Winds has four scouts out front on point, but none back as a rear guard. The last Nez Perce warrior walking is lagging behind about fifty feet from his nearest Nez Perce warrior, when a huge paw with long claws strikes him in the head and knocks him dead, like a fish that floats on its side and Sun Man catches him before he hits the ground and makes any noise. What a war weapon, these two powerful beings make, as they began to take more Nez Perce fighters in this manner.

The Nez Perce war party moves forward, unaware they are under attack from the rear. More than twenty have been taken down, before one brave has stopped to acesli (to urinate – Lakota dialect) and sees the great waowešica (a bear, in general) attack an unsuspecting fellow warrior, and he sounds the alarm.

Sun Man motions off Mato Hota Brother and unseen, he falls back as well. They both leave and head back to the pass at a good pace, leaving the Nez Perce far behind and in a state of utter confusion, finding many bodies of their warriors strewn around, all with terrible wounds, that took their lives in silence.

Chief Walking Winds, gathers his warriors and covers the dead with rocks, gathers their weapons and sends out many scouts in all directions within a half mile distance. They are ordered to go no further and return and let him know if there is any sign of the great bear that killed them and most of all, he would like to know why a bear would attack all these warriors.

All the scouts return, with no answers, except one, a great scout of twenty-five seasons, who has tracked many animals before, has found the tracks of Mato Hota Brother and saw signs he was running east at a fast pace, as the tracks told him. This report did not mean anything of importance to the young chief, as the great bear, could have gone in any direction to flee from his many warriors.

He would have a rear guard of ten braves watch the rear of his advancing warriors. He moved forward as planned, but this is a troubling omen and his spirit is low. The young chief cannot let his warriors know he is troubled, for they look to him for strength and guidance and he is wise enough to show no fear to them.

The Nez Perce force moves to the beginning of the pass. When Nez Perce braves hear a great noise of something unknown tearing through the tops of tree behind the rear guard, they are frightened. It sounds like the world is falling behind them and many Nez Perce braves run forward away from these crashing noises. Soon, the air is carrying round rocks hitting many enemy braves, like huge hail stones coming in horizontally and from other angles. When these rocks hit trees, many smaller ones are broken down, when they hit men, they are killed or injured. Some rocks kill more than one man, with the force of travel, they possess.

Sun Man is throwing rocks in rapid succession, with his mighty arm. He is raining more than river rocks on them by his attack, he is raining terror of the unknown upon them and that is true terror, a terror one cannot fight with bows and arrow or spears. The Nez Perce, still have not seen any sign of a human enemy and can only move further into the pass or stay in place.

Chief Walking Winds, orders twenty braves to try to go around the pass to the north and twenty to the south, to scout a way around this area. The northern band reaches an area, that clears into a small opening and when they enter, they come under a hail of arrows from Oyaka and his Coast Salish Flathead warriors. Many are taken down, but more charge forward and the hand to hand fighting begins in earnest.

A big Nez Perce brave launches an attack on Oyaka, with a tomahawk and he side steps him and jabs his spear deep into the side of the attacker, who goes down with his spear buried deep in his side, screaming in pain. Next, Oyaka pulls his knife and charges an enemy, that has pinned another Coast Salish Flathead warrior to the ground and is about to club him with his hatchet. He stops the hatchet blow and stabs his knife into the neck of the Nez Perce wounding him, he drops his hatchet and grabs his throat with both hands, but he cannot stop the blood from flowing and passes out, as death comes to claim his youth, he will have no children with his new wife, such is the risk of war. No Nez Perce return from their mission north to report to their chief.

The Nez Perce band sent to the south, are surprise by Okolaya and his braves and the great mato hota has attacked five of the twenty, killing them all, with swipes of his big paws. The rest fight with fear and are easily defeated. Okolaya shoots arrows into two with his keen eye and wantanyeya (be skillful in shooting – Lakota dialect) training for battle. He is a proven warrior. All enemy weapons are gathered up, after the dead are stacked together and covered with brush. No one is left alive of the Nez Perce, to report back to their young chief.

The Nez Perce chief, is pinned down in place with his warriors hiding behind any trees or boulders they find to shelter them from the deadly barrage of river rocks, that periodically come crashing in on them. So far, the war plan of the Coast Salish Flathead chief and Wanagiyata, has worked perfectly, along with Sun Man and Mato Hota Brother's help. The main body of Nez Perce warriors are pinned down, and have no way to go, but through the pass. Night is falling and this is the time, that the young chief, thinks he can move his warriors away from this unknown attack upon his warriors. As darkness sets in, he gives the signal for his men to move through the pass.

As all the Nez Perce move into the pass and are half way though, big rocks come thundering down upon them from high above. These big rocks come from both sides of the pass and many screams break the silence of night. The avalanche of rocks and small boulders rain down on each end of the pass blocking it by boulders on the eastern end. Oyaka and his warriors group up with Okolaya's warriors and climb up on the blockage of boulders on the west end of the pass, which block any retreat from the fleeing Nez Perce warriors.

When the avalanche stops, many screams for help come from many of the living. It is a long night of suffering for many and those who are alive, are hiding among the fallen boulders afraid to move in their blind trap. Even still, no enemy man has been seen by Chief Walking Winds or his living warriors and fear is the enemy he faces, along with his right arm crushed by a big boulder and he is trapped and has passed out many times during the long night.

He wakes up and he sees three šungmanitu breathing their hot breath on him. He screams for help, but there is none coming from his few living warriors, about thirty have fled toward the west end of the pass and been captured by Oyaka and Okolaya and their forty warriors, along with the help of Mato Hota Brother. They surrendered without a fight and were easily disarmed and held in place.

Chief Buffalo Finder and Wanagiyata have entered to the east end of the pass after, Sun Man, has cleared the rock rubble. Wanagiyata finds his three wolf scouts standing over the trapped young defeated Nez Perce Chief. The wolf brothers back away from the chief, who is totally terrified by them, thinking he will be eaten alive with his arm crushed under a big boulder.

Chief Buffalo Finder, Wanagiyata, and Sun Man approach the stricken Nez Perce warrior chief. Wanagiyata, speaks to him in Nez Perce dialect, "Where is your chief young warrior, I would speak with him?" "He is dead unless this rock is lift off me, and I will die from my wound, as my blood flows from me, answers," Chief Walking Winds.

Sun Man lifts the large boulder off the young Nez Perce and Wanagiyata kneels beside him. "Do you wish to go in peace, if you are freed"? asks Wanagiyata. The young chief is amazed at the strength of Sun Man and cannot believe he was also, saved from wolves by these strangers, who must be wakan (holy) to be so powerful. He agrees in sign by nodding his head yes without speaking wasted words.

Wanagiyata lowers his head and prays over the young chief foe a healing of his crushed arm. Wanagiyata says, "Rise up and be whole." The Nez Perce Chief feels his numbed arm wake up and all his feeling returns to his arm and he makes a fist and relaxes it and he stands up and looks into the eyes of Wanagiyata. He sees ionšilaya (having compassion on one – Lakota dialect) and woonšila (mercy – Lakota dialect) in his eyes and drops to his knees in honor of this fine man who heals and does not kill his enemy when he is helpless, but rather saves him and offers to free him. The young chief says, "What would you have me do, great one"? "You will camp with us, after I heal all your wounded men and they will join us and I will tell you a story for all time, for now, follow me," says Wanagiyata.

 Wakantanka (God) has given Wanagiyata his healing powers and he goes around and finds forty more wounded and near-death Nez Perce warriors, and heals them all to the joy of Chief Walking Winds. All the Nez Perce prisoners are reunited with the healed survivors and camp is made and a celebration is given for a great victory, but the Nez Perce are treated as guest not prisoners.

After the meal and celebration has concluded, Wanagiyata speaks after Chief Buffalo Finder has spoken words of thanks to his braves for their bravery and following the war plan he and

Wanagiyata, along with Sun Man's ideas, worked perfectly. Wanagiyata tells the great story of the 'Two Earths' and is told all the Nez Perce become believers. Sun Man is asked to move a large boulder near camp and this is done, before he tells most of his story to the entire camp. All are amazed by this and know in their mind and heart that Wakantanka and His Son, Tatanka Ska Son, loves them and they are all believers.

The Nez Perce warriors leave for their village after recovering their dead or some item from them for family to hold, after learning of their location from Wanagiyata. They will return with many stories to share, as they have become 'Story Tellers'. The young chief, has a new understanding of the Coast Salish Flathead people and will return to his village and heal the wounds of hatred, that have been passed down for centuries and mourn for their dead. The Coast Salish Flathead are now dakotas (allies or friends) to them.

The Coast Salish Flathead mission of war is a complete success and not one warrior has been lost. The return trip to the Coast Salish Flathead village seems to take a long time, but that is the feeling of Sun Man, more than all others, because he is ready to take on a marriage to the beautiful daughter of Chief Buffalo Finder when he returns.

While most of the men in the Coast Salish Flathead village have gone to war, the women of the village have run the daily lives of those remaining older Coast Salish Flathead and all children, as they are the backbone of the village life. Wachiwi (dancing girl), Gidagaakoons (fawn – Chippewa dialect), and Kimimila (butterfly) have been helping with wedding plans for their friend and bride to be Blossom Flowers. Blossom Flowers is very excited to see Sun Man, her father and learn that all Coast

Salish Flathead braves have returned safely. A great celebration takes place for two days before the wedding for Sun Man and Blossom Flowers, arrives.

The day of the wedding, the weather is clear and fair, with intermittent clouds in the sky. When all have gathered together as witnesses to this most special of marriages, a joining of the Coast Salish Flathead tribe to the Crow tribe and thereby, makes them dakotas to the Oglala Lakota tribe by this eminent union. It is certain the tribes will be dakotas as witnessed in this moment of much joy and excitement, which is shared by all present. Chief Buffalo Finder is to say a few words and give his daughter away to Sun Man, but just as he calls for silence, by raising both hands up high toward Wakantanka's Lodge, the sky grows darker.

Soon, as all look in wonder and awe, a bright blue and white tunnel of light appears in the western sky and moves over them and circles around the Coast Salish Flathead village. Wanagiyata and his companions know what is happening and are thrilled,

knowing their Itancanka (the chief one, lord and master) is coming again to them. Many of the Coast Salish Flathead know from the 'Story Tellers', about Tatanka Ska Son (Son of Wakantanka) and now they will see Him in person again. The tunnel of light lands behind Chief Buffalo Finder and now all face the tunnel of light, as Tatanka Ska Son appears. The chief motions all to kneel and everyone is kneeling, as Tatanka Ska Son speaks, "Stand My brothers and sisters, I come to show My respect and love for you and to perform the first wedding blessed by Wakantanka, He who has sent Me to do so. Step forward Sun Man with Blossom Flowers."

Sun Man and Blossom Flowers walk hand in hand up to Tatanka Ska Son and stand facing Him. Tatanka Ska Son speaks loud enough for all to hear His Voice, "Blossom Flowers, speak words from your heart to this man, that he may know your heart is true. Sun Man, speak words from your heart to this maiden, that she may know your heart is true." Blossom Flowers, looks deep into Sun Man's eyes and says, "I will honor you for all my days. I will serve you with my works. I will serve you with my heart and never, will I speak against you forever. Your life is my life, your God is my God and I will love you both until my breath is no more."

Sun Man is deeply moved by the words of Blossom Flowers and pauses for a long moment, turning some heads, as some Coast Salish Flathead villagers look at each other, as if to be puzzled, that he would not speak, as was asked of him by Tatanka Ska Son in this wedding ceremony. At last Sun Man speaks, "Blossom Flowers, you honor me standing with me before my Savior, Tatanka Ska Son, Son of Wakantanka, my God. It is He who has given me great strength to save you from the giant golden mato hota and it is He who gave Wanagiyata the powers to heal you to be my bride this day. Your words have touched my heart and will live forever in my mind. All that you have spoken, I give back to you in words and deeds. May we give children to serve Wakantanka and have His Blessings in our lodge forever as the sun warms Mother Earth."

Tatanka Ska Son, scratches the ground before Him and smoke rises in the air and is replaced by a halo of bright white light, which fades and in its place revealing a small bed of pine needles, with two rings made by Tatanka Ska Son. He continues, "Sun Man, give one to your bride, as a gift of love to wear on this earth. Blossom Flowers, give one to Sun Man to wear in this life. These rings are round, as a circle, a symbol of never-ending love and made of gold, which never tarnishes or rots. Place one on Blossom Flowers finger, near to her smallest finger of her left hand. Blossom Flowers, take the other ring and place it on Sun Man's finger." Sun Man places the small ring on Blossom Flowers slender finger, and then Blossom Flowers, repeats in the same manner.

Tatanka Ska Son says, "This is My first marriage to Bless and I do so with great joy in My heart. Go in love with your wife Sun Man, she is yours and you are hers forever on Mother Earth. Love and serve My Father, Wakantanka, and He will watch over you with His love. Go now as husband and wife, it is a good thing. Before I return to My Father's side, I bless all in this village this day." Tatanka Ska Son lifts off and flies away at high speed and disappears into the sun.

Sun Man and Blossom Flowers turn and face everyone gathered for their wedding. A great swell of cheering and chanting break the still silence. This night will be the best Chief Buffalo Finder and his wife, Running Waters, could provide, with many gifts given to all the Coast Salish Flathead villagers and it's 'Story Tellers'. Many gifts are given to Sun Man and his new wife Blossom Flowers. Wanagiyata, gives a šunkawakan to Sun Man for his wife to ride by his side and both are thrilled by this most wonderful gift, few have seen this far west, much less own.

Two days have passed and after a fine meal, singing, and dancing have been enjoyed by all. Some young maidens dance dances taught to them by Wachiwi and they perform very well. Wanagiyata stands after asking for the right to speak from the chief. All goes silent and all present want their ears to hear Wanagiyata's words. "My dear dakotas, my words I speak to you are heavy to carry and I must give them to all listening. My 'Story Tellers' and I must take our mission of 'Story Telling' northwest to the tribes who dwell there and worship poles of wood and evil spirits of the mind.

"We will miss the dakota's made here in your village and will return to your tipis (teepee or lodge or tent) and warm fires when we return down the Great River," says Wanagiyata. The hush among the villagers is broken by some sad words spoken among many, but they do understand the 'Story Tellers' have a mission to spread the Words and Wishes of Wakantanka and heal the sick and suffering, wherever they go.

The entire village helps, with the provisioning of the raft and provides buffalo hides for extra sleeping use, and cover the small cabin onboard the raft. They make extra ropes from tree fiber they know how to use for that purpose. The Coast Salish Flathead people are very knowledgeable about plants and herbs, and have taught Kimimila, Gidagaakoons and Wachiwi many ways to identify them and their uses. Fortunate for all the 'Story Tellers', that now Blossom Flowers is part of their mission.

One of the big gifts Chief Buffalo Finder has given to Sun Man and Wanagiyata is a scout, who has been up river hundreds of miles, before being attacked by Pend d'Oreille (also known as Kalispel) Indians. They shot arrows at him from the river bank, while he was in his canoe and he had to turn and race away and return back to the Coast Salish Flathead village. Other great gifts were given to each brave among the 'Story Tellers' one of which was a birch bark canoe, which would be most useful, for scouting and giving them the ability to be anchored out in the river, and use the canoe to go to shore or scout ahead for trouble on the water or on shore. These Coast Salish Flathead birch bark canoes are very sturdy and tough, made with great skill and craftsmanship, by few with this knowledge.

Chief Buffalo Finder and his dear wife, Running Waters, have tears wetting their cheeks, as they wave farewell to their daughter, Blossom Flowers, and her new husband, Sun Man, now their mighty son by marriage. The fully loaded raft is pulled by the šunkawakans from shore, as they disappear from sight going northwest up the Great River.

We leave our 'Story Tellers' resuming their mission traveling northwest on the Great River toward more adventures and Campfire Stories to come in book three, <u>River Dangers Lie Ahead</u> in the series of "The Chosen Ones Oglala Warriors." Until, then study your Lakota words and may your hearts and actions follow Wakantanka. May you always be blessed, for you are so special to Tatanka Ska Son, Who loves you.

Appendix

ALPHABETICAL BOOK TWO LAKOTA
AND
OTHER MEANINGS
Most meanings of words in Lakota dialect came from the Lakota
dictionary using their Lakota alphabetical system of order and
English alphabetical form – Lakota-English/ English-Lakota
New Comprehensive Edition; Compiled and Edited by Eugene
Buechel and Paul Manhart
University of Nebraska Press, 2002.

a·book·sig·un \a-book-sig-un\ (wildcat – Chippewa dialect)

a·can·te·šil·ya·kel \a-can-te-šil-ya-k̇el\ (sadly or sorrowfully for)

a·ce·sli \a-cé-sli\ (to urinate)

a·gi·ci·da \a-gi-ci-da\ (soldier; Camp Watcher – Assiniboine dialect)

a·hin·han \a-híṇ-haṇ\ (to rain upon, to fall as rain does on things)

a·i·glu·ho·mni \a-i-glu-ho-mni\ (to turn on, to throw one's self at, as in battle)

a·i·kpa·bla·ya \a-í-kpa-bla-ya\ (to make a fool of one's self by talking or acting foolishly)

a·i·tan·can \a-í-taṇ-caṇ\ (the ruler over)

a·ki·ta one \a-k̇í-ṫa\ (to seek or hunt for, as something lost, determined and never give up) (first or single – English language)

a·ki·ta two \a-kí-ta\ (to seek or hunt for, as something lost, determined and never give up) (two – second or one plus one = two – English language)

Al·gon·qu·ian \al-gon-qu-ian\ (a member of a North American Indian people living in Canada along the Ottawa River and its tributaries and westward to the north Lake Superior – source SIRI)

am·i·to·la \am-i-to-la\ (rainbow – Chippewa dialect)

an·imi·kii \an-imi-kii\ (thunder – Animaikii is a giant mythological thunder-bird common to the northern and western tribes. Thunder is caused by the beating of their immense wings - in Chippewa dialect) – **wa·kin·yan** \wa-kín-yan\ (thunder, the cause and source of thunder and lightning, once supposed by Dakota to be a great bird).

Ani·xshin·áabe \Ani-xshin-áabe\ (is the autonym for a group of culturally related indigenous people residing in what are now Canada and the United States. These also include the Odawa, Saulteaux, Ojibwe (including Mississaugas), Potawatomi, Oji-Cree, and Algonquin people. The Anishinaabe means "original person." The Anixshináabe speak many different dialects, as they have many tribes)

Anishinaabemowin or Anishináabe languages that belong to the Algonquian language family. They historically lived in the Northeast Woodlands and Subarctic. – Source, 'Wikipedia'

a·nun·ka·san \a-núŋ-ka-saŋ\ (bald or white-headed eagle)

A·pache \Ə'-paSH\ (a member of a North American people living chiefly in New Mexico and Arizona. The Apache put up fierce resistance to the European settlers and were, under the leadership of Geronimo, the last American Indian people to be conquered)

Aps·á·a·look·e \Aps-á-a-look-e\ (The Crow in Siouan dialect – meaning – "children of the large-beaked bird")

ari·ka·ra \ari-ka-ra\ (running wolf – Crow dialect)

aspiitu' \aspiitu'\ (claw – Pawnee dialect)

A·ss·in·i·bo·ine \A-ss-in-i-bo-ine\ (Assiniboine or Assiniboine people when singular when plural; Ojibwe Asiniibwaan, "stone Sioux"; also known as the Hole and known by the endonym Nakota (or Nakoda or Nakona), are First Nations/Native American people originally from the Great Plain of North America - Wikipeda)

A·tha·bas·kan \A-tha-bas-kan\ (A family of American Indian languages spoken primarily in western Canada, Alaska, and the Southwest – Some Western Apache use this language)

a·wa·ci \a-wá-ca\ (to dance on anything or in honor of)

a·wa·ši·ca·ho·wa·ya \a-wa-ši-cá-ho-wa-ya\ (to cry out on account of)

axxa·ash·e \axxa-ash-e\ (sun – Crow dialect)

a·yu·hla·gan \a-yú-ħla-ġaŋ\ (to make large upon)

baax·peé \baax-pee\ (power transcending the ordinary – Crow dialect)

ba·ch·hee \ba-ch-hee\ (man – Crow – dialect)

bag·wun·gi·ji·k \bag-wun-gi-ji-k\ (hole in the sky – Chippewa dialect)

bas·axe \bas-axe\ (turtle – Crow dialect)

bii·lee \bii-lee\ (swan – Crow dialect)

bi'shee \bi'shee\ (buffalo – Crow dialect)

bla·ya \blá-ya\ (level, plain)

blo·ki·t'a \bló-ki-t'a\ (to be very tired, weary, exhausted)

bow \bow\ (the bow is the forward part of the ship or boat, the point that is usually most forward when the vessel is underway m- English language)

bua \bua\ (fish – Crow dialect)

ca·ch·e \ca-ch-e\ (a collection of items of the same type stored in a hidden or unaccessible place – French language)

can·ška \can-šká\ (red-legged hawk, the large white-breasted hawk, a snake eater)

can·te·ki·ya \can-té-ki-ya\ (to love, to have an interest in or affection for, which prompts one to perform benevolent acts)

can·te·yu·kan \can̞-té-yu-kan\ (to have heart, to be benevolent)

can·to·gna·gya \can̞-tó-gna-gya\ (in a loving manner)

ca·pa \cá-p̣a\ (beaver)

ce·tan tan·ka \ca-tan\ (a hawk) tanka \tan-ka\ (large, great in any way) cetan tanka (the big hawk)

che·é·te \che-é-te\ (wolf – Crow dialect)

Chi·nook \Chi-nook\ (are a small American Indian Tribe, speaking a Chinookan dialect and are located around the mouth of the Columbia River, Clackamas and Willamette Rivers in Oregon)

Chip·pe·wa \chip-pe-wa\ (The names Chippewa, Ojibway, Ojibwe, Ojibwa all come from an Algonquin word, which means "puckered," mostly because of the shape of their moccasins and how they appeared. The Ojibway call themselves Anishináabe meaning 'original person', all are people of Canada and the United States of America.)

chogan \chogan\ (blackbird – Algonquin dialect)

ci·k'a·la \ċi-k'a-la\ (little, very small) –"When used as one word"

cin·ca \ciŋ-cà\ (a child, the young of animals)

ci·qa·la \ċi-q'a-la\ (little one)

Coast Salish \Co-ast Sa-lish\ (the Coast Salish is a group of ethnically and Linguistically related Indigenous people of the Pacific Northwest Coast, living in British Columbia, Canada and the U.S. states of Washington and Oregon. They speak one of the Coast Salish languages – Wikipedia)

co·k'in \co-k'iŋ\ (to roast on spits over coals)

Crow \Crow\ (The Crow, called the Apsáalooke in their own Siouan language, or variants including the Absaroka, are Native Americans, who in historical times lived in the Yellowstone Valley, which extends from present-day Wyoming though Montana and into North Dakota, where it joins the Missouri River)

dakota \dakota\ (allies or friends)

e·han·na \e-háŋ-na\ (long ago)

e·ki·ci·pa \é-ki-ci-pa\ (to meet and attack)

fire brand \fire brand\ (a burning torch – English language)
petuspe (a fire brand – Lakota dialect)

Gidagaakoons \gidagaakoons\ (fawn – Chippewa dialect)

glu·ha \glu-há\ (to have or possess one's own)

gun·ga \ġúŋ-ġa\ (proud, with eyes closed not minding others, haughty)

gun·gaga·ya\ġúŋ-ġa-ġa-ya\ (proudly)

ha \ha\ (the skin or hide of animal)

ha·ho ha·ho \ha-hó ha-hó\ (express of joy on receiving something)

ha·ci·la \ha-ċí-la\ (children)

han·pa \háŋ-ṗa\ (moccasin)

ha·pa·šlo·ka \ha-ṗá-šlo-ka\ (to pull off skin, to chafe)

ha·yu·za \há-yu-za\ (to skin, take off the skin of anything)

he·han·han·ke·ca \he-háŋ-haŋ-ke-ca\ (each so long)

he·ha·ka \he-há-ka\ (the male elk, so called from its branching horns)

he·hak i·kto·mi \he-hák i-któ-mi\ (a moose)

he·ton \he-tón\ (horned) cik'ala \cí-k'a-la\ - heton cikala (an antelope)

he·yu·ḣa \he-yú-ḣa\ (the name of animals with branching horns)

hi·a·ki·gle \hi-á-ki-gle\ (to set the teeth firmly)

hin·sko \hín-sko\ (so big, so large)

hin·to \hin-to\ (gray horse)

ho·gle·gle·ga \ho-glé-gle-ġa\ (the grass pike, or the rainbow fish)

hom·me \hom-me\ (man – Apache dialect)

hu \hu\ (the leg of man)

hui·ya·kas·kes \huí-ya-kas-kes\ (ankle ornaments for Sundance)

ḣo·ka \ḣo-ḱá\ (badger)

h'e·h'e·ya \ḣ'e-ḣ'é-ya\ (slobbering)

hunga \hunga\ (tribal chief – Assiniboine dialect)

hungabi \hungabi\ (little chiefs – Assiniboine dialect)

i·gla·s·to \i-glá-s-to\ (to be left out, incomplete)

i·glu·wan·ka·tu·ya \i-glú-waṇ-ka-tu-ya\ (to elevate or raise up one's self, over others, i. e. to be proud)

i·gmu·watogla \i-gmú-watogla\ (mountain lion)

i·gni \i-gní\ (to hunt, seek for, to follow after e.g. game)

ii·ch·ii·le \ii-ch-ii-le\ (horse – Crow dialect)

i·kpi \i-kṗí\ (belly)

i·o·ma·ka \í-o-ma-ka\ (the year next to, the next year - time)

ionšilaya \i-óŋ-ši-la\ (having compassion on one)

i·tan·can·ka \i-táŋ-caŋ-ka\ (the chief one, lord and master)

i·to·ke·ca \i-tó-ke-ca\ (to be altered, changed, to be affected by in any way)

i·tun·psi·ca·la \i-túŋ-psi-ca-la\ (the field mouse)

i·wa·gla·mna \i-wá-gla-mna\ (an extra or fresh horse)

i·wan·gla·ka \i-wáŋ-gla-ka\ (to look to, have regard for one's own)

i·wa·to·han·tu \í-wa-to-haŋ-tu\ (sometime, one day in reference to something)

i·ya·ki·ta \í-ya-ki-ta\ (to have an eye to, keep watch on)

i·ya·pa \i-ya-pa\ (a snow storm)

i·ya·š'a·pi \í-ya-š'à-pi\ (an acclamation)

i·ye·han \i-yé-haŋ\ (at the appointed time)

iyeya \iyeya\ (quickness or suddenness)

jer·ky \jer-ky\ (smoked dried meat – in English language)

Jicarilla Apache \JI-ca-rill-a A-pa-che\ (Jicarilla Apache, one of several loosely organized autonomous bands of the Eastern Apache, refers to members of the Jicarilla Apache Nation currently living in New Mexico and speaking a Southern Athabaskan language)

ka·ga·pa \ka-ġá-pa\ (to cut, spread open by cutting, to lay open)

ka·lu·za \ka-lú-za\ (to flow rapidly, as water)

214

kan·gi·ha mi·gna·ka \k̇aŋ-ġí-ha mi-gnà-ka\ (a feather disk, resembling the unhcela kagapi)

kan·htal \káŋ-ḣtal\ (relaxed, with a loss of tension)

ka·psan·psan \k̇a-psáŋ-psaŋ\ (to dangle, swing back and forth, to sway to and fro, as a limb in the water)

ka·tka \ká-tka\ (briskly)

kes·ton \k̇es-ṫón\ (a barbed arrowhead)

ki·ca·mna·yan \k̇i-cá-mna-yaŋ\ (in an overwhelming way)

ki·can \k̇i-cáŋ\ (cries out loudly)

ki·mi·mi·la \k̇i-mí-mi-la\ (butterfly)

ki·tan·yan·kel \ k̇i-táŋ-yaŋ-k̇el\ (with the greatest difficulty)

ko·ška·la \ko-šká-la\ (a young man)

ku·ka \k̇u-ká\ (rotten, spoiled, as meat, tender, worn out, as clothes)

kukuše \kukuše\ (pig)

kuúruks \kuúruks\ (bear – Pawnee dialect)

La·ko·ta \La-ko-ta\ (Lakota, Nakota and Dakota are the names of three larger Siouan people living generally in the north-central United States of America)

lu·za·han \lú-za-haŋ\ (swift, to be fast, fast running)

ma·hpi·hpi·ya \ma-ḣpí-ḣpi-ya\ (scattered clouds)

Ma·hpi·ya \ma-ḣpí-ya\ (Heaven, the clouds, the afterlife of mankind)

mahtowitko \mahtowitko\ (Crazy Bear – Assiniboine dialect)

ma'·i·ing·an \ma'-i-ing-an\ (timber wolf – Chippewa dialect)

ma·ka \ma-ḱá\ (skunk or pole cat)

ma·ko·k'e \ma-k̄ō'-k'e\ (a dug-out, a pit)

ma·to cin·ca·la \ma-tó ciṇ-cà-la\ (bear cub)

ma·to ḣo·ta \ma-tó ḣò-ta\ (the grizzly bear)

ma·tos·kah \ma-tos-kah\ (white bear)

metate \me-ta-te\ (a flat or slightly hollowed oblong stone on which materials such as grain and cocoa are ground using a smaller stone – Mexican origin – English language)

mi·gna·ka \mi-gná-k̇a\ (to put in under the girdle)

mni \mi-ní\ (water)

mor·tars \mor-tars\ (a mortar is shaped like a bowl and made of stone – English language)

na·gi \na-ġí\ (the soul or spirit)

na·pe·on·wo·gla·ka \na-ṗé-oṇ-wò-gla-ka\ (sign, signs, signing – to use sign language – to communicate using gestures with hands or other body movement and facial expressions)

na·tan \na-ṫáṇ\ (to make an attack, to go after and rush upon e.g. the enemy)

na·wi·zi \na-wí-zi\ (to be jealous or envious)

ndolkan \n-dol-kan\ (cougar – Apache dialect)

ni·štu·šte \ni-štú-šte\ (the rump)

o·ce·sli \o-cé-sli\ (to defecate in)

O·gla·la \O-glá-la\ (scatter one's own – name of one of three larger clans of the Teton Sioux Indian people living in the north-central United States of America)

o·gli·gle wa·kan \o-glí-gle wa-kan\ (a good angel)

o·glu \o-glú\ (luck, fortune)

o·ha·mna \o-há-mna\ (smelling of skin – to smell badly)

o·i·pu·ta·ke \o-í-pu-ta-ke\ (kiss)

o·ji·la·ka \ó-ji-la-ka\ (the offspring, the young one's of both men and animals)

o·kan·šni·yan \o-kán-šni-yaŋ\ (having no time)

o·ki·t'a \o-kí-t'a\ (to be tired, fatigued or worn out by)

okiwinja \o-kí-wiŋ-ja\ (to bind down thoroughly)

o·ki·yu·ta \ó-ki-yu-ta\ (to heal up)

okizi·wa·ki·ya \o-ki-zi-wa-ki-ya\ (to cause to heal up)

okolaya \o-kó-la-ya\ (to have as a friend)

O·ma·ha \O-ma-ha\ (The Omaha Indian people are from the Upper Missouri River – Omaha in their dialect means – flat water)

on·ši·la \óŋ-ši-la\ (to have mercy on)

o·ta·ku·ye \o-tá-ku-ye\ (brotherhood, relationship, relations, kinfolk, kinship)

o·wa·mni·o·mni \o-wá-mni-o-mni\ (an eddy, whirl-pool, a cyclone)

o·wo·gla·ke \o-wó-gla-ke\ (a council chamber to consult or confer)

oyaka \oyaka\ (to tell, report, relate)

o·ya·te \o-yá-te\ (a people, nation, tribe, or band)

pa·e \pa-é\ (to inflict punishment in order to prevent future lapses)

pa·ta·ka \pa-tá-ka\ (to come to a stand as a horse does)

Pend d'Oreille \Pend d'Oreille\ (The **Pend d'Oreille**, also known as the **Kalispel**, are Indigenous peoples of the Northwest Plateau. Today many of them live in Montana and eastern Washington.- Wikipedia)

pes·tle \pes-tle\ (a pestle is aa blunt stone or stick used to pound seeds or grain into a mortar to crush and grind them into meal – English language)

peša \pé-ša\ (the headgear used in the Omaha dance, and made of the porcupine skin, the Omahas being the first to use it)

pe·ti·le·ya·pi \pe-tí-le-ya-pi\ (kindling)

pe·tka·i·le s'e \pe-tká-i-le s'e\ (in the manner of fanning a fire to life by adding wood)

pe·tu·spe \pe-tú-spe\ (a firebrand with which to start a fire)

port \po-rt\ (left side – English language used in Nautical terms)

port·a·ging \port-a-ging\ (carrying a canoe or boat – French/Canadian dialect)

powwow (a North American Indian gathering ceremony involving feasting, singing, dancing, and trading)

ptan \ptaŋ\ (the otter)

pte·ha·šla \pte-há-šla\ (a buffalo hide from which the hair has been removed)

pte·he wa·pa·ha \ptehé wa-pà-ha\ (horned headgear)

pte·o·pta·ye \pte-ó-pta-ye\ (a buffalo herd)

sa·ke·hans·ka \sa-ke-hans-ka\ (a grizzly bear)

ska \ska\ (white)

sin·te·han·ska \siŋ-ṫé-han-ska\ (whitetail deer)

sin·te·sa·pe·la \siŋ-ṫé-sa-ṗe-la\ (black-tail deer or mule deer)

ša·ke·hu·te s'e hin·gle \ša-ḱé-hu-ṫe s'e hiŋ-gle\ (angry as a bear)

ši·ca·ho·wa·wa \ši-cá-ho-wa-wa\ (to cry out)

Si·oux La·ko·ta \Si-oux La-ḱó-ṫa\ (Lakota, Nakota, and Dakota are the names of three of the larger Siouan people living generally in the north-central United States of America)

son (son) (a boy or man in relation to either or both of his parents – English language)

Sun Man \sun man\ (in English language) Wica \wi-ca\ (man – in Lakota dialect) of wiyóhiyanpa \wi-yo-hi-yan-pa\ (the east, raising sun – in Lakota dialect) or Axxaashe \axxa-ash-e\ (sun – Crow dialect) Bachhee \ba-ch-hee\ (man – in Crow dialect)

stone \stone\ (throw stones at – English language)

Sun·dance \Sun-dance\ (Sundance – English language (Wiwanyank Wacipi – Lakota dialect)

šun·gblo·ka \šuṇ-gbló-ka\ (the male horse or dog)

šun·gi·la \šuṇ-ġí-la\ (the fox)

šun·gma·ni·tu \šuṇ-gmá-ni-ṭu\ (a wolf)

šun·gma·ni·tu ai·tan·can \šuṇ-gmá-ni-ṭu ai-táṇ-can-ḳa\ (wolf ruler)

šun·gwin·ye·la \šuṇ-gwíṇ-ye-la\ (a mare horse – female horses)

šun·ka \šún-ḳa\ (a dog)

šun·ka·wa·kan \šúṇ-ḳa-wa-kan\ (a horse)

šun·ka·wa·kan ta·wa·na·p'in \šúṇ-ḳa-wa-kaṇ ta-wa-nà-p'in\ (a horse collar)

šun·kma·ni·tu \šuṇ·kmá-ni-ṭu\ (a coyote)

šun'·on·k'on·pa \šuṇ-óṇ-k'oṇ-pa\ (pony or dog travois, drag, the original vehicle of the Dakotas displaced by the wagon, the former consisting of two poles, one pair of ends fastened together and placed on the back of the pony or dog with a strap around the breast, the other pair of ends dragging over the ground. The baggage rested on the 'šunktacangleška' baggage basket which is tied across the poles behind the tail of the horse or dog)

šu·ška \ šu-šká\ (tardy)

symbi·osis \symbi-osis\ (inter action between two different organisms living in close physical association, typically to the advantage of both – German and New Latin from the Greek origin)

ta·blo·ka \ta-bló-ka\ (a buck, the male of the common deer)

ta·ha \ta-há\ (a deerskin)

ta·ha·ka·la·la \ta-há-ka-la-la\ (a women's buckskin dress, usually fringed, etc.)

ta·ha·lo \ta-há-lo\ (a hide)

ta·ha·pe wa·po·štan \ta-há-p̣e wa-p̣ò-štaɳ\ (a cap made of buffalo fur with the hair outside)

ta·hu·hu·te \ta-hú-hu-ṫe\ (nape of the neck)

ta·ḣca \ṫá-ḣca\ (deer – venison)

ta·kan \ta-káɳ\ (sinew taken from the back of a deer, buffalo, or cow which is used for thread)

ta·ki·yu·ḣa \ta-k̇í-yu-ḣa\ (any bull of cattle, deer, etc)

ta·ko·da \ta-ko-da\ (friend to everyone)

ta·ko·laku \ta-k̇ó-laka\ (his special friend)

ta·kpe \ta-kp̣é\ (to come upon, attack; make an attack)

ta·ku·ya \ṫa·k̇ú-ya\ (to have one for a relation)

tan·ka \táɳ-ka\ (large, great in any way)

tan·ni·ka \taṇ-ní-k̇a\ (old, worn out, ancient, archaic)

ta·tan·ka \ta-táṇ-k̇a\ (a male buffalo)

ta·tan·ka ha \ta-táṇ-k̇a ha\ (buffalo skin or hide with hair)

ta·tan·ka ska \ta-táṇ-k̇a ska\ (white buffalo)

Ta·tan·ka Ska Son \Ta-táṇ-k̇a Ska Son\ (a male buffalo, white, a man – Son of God Tatanka Ska Son – Jesus Christ Son of God, in the form of a white buffalo)

ta·wa·kpe ya \ta-wa-kpe ya\ (to go to attacking)

ta·wi·cu \ta-wí-cu\ (his wife)

ta·wi·cu·wa·ton \ta-wí-cu-wa-ton\ (to be married)

tarry (to delay or be tardy in acting or doing – English language)

tethered (tie an animal with rope or chain so as to restrict its movement)

Te·ton \Te-ton\ (another term for Lakota)

Te·ton Si·oux \Te-ton Si-oux\ (name of the Lakota people and the Nakota and Dakota bands)

Till·a·mook (Tillamook \Till-a-mook\ (among the Indian tribes who inhabited the Oregon coast were the Tillamock.In historical reports, the name "Tillamook" is also spelled Killemuck, Kilamox, Callemex, and Killimux. The name roughly means "those who live at Nehalem" and was applied to all of the Salish-speaking Indians south of the Clatsops and lived usually by the mouth of rivers, most especially during the winter - Wikipedia)

ti·pi \tí-ṗi\ (teepee or tent or lodge)

ti·ta·ku·ye \tí-ta-k̇u-ye\ (the immediate relatives)

ti·wa·he \ti-wá-he\ (a household, i.e. including persons as well as things)

T·lin·git (\T-lin-git\ (the Tlingit are indigenous people of the Pacific Northwest Coast of North America. Their language is Tlingit, in which the name means "People of the tides" - Wikipeda)

to·ka \ṫó-k̇a\ (one of a foreign or hostile nation, an enemy)

to·ka·ta \to-k̇á-ta\ (in the future, or the future)

to·ke·ke·kel \ṫo-k̇é-k̇e-kel\ (with ripe concernedness)

to·la·hca·ka \tō'-la-ḣca· k̇a\ (very blue)

to·ma·hawk \to-ma-hawk\ (the tomahawk originated from the Algonquin Indians of the Sioux Nation. The word came from the words tamahak or tamahakan. The Native American Indians regularly used tomahawks made from stone heads which were attached to wooden handles and tied with strips of rawhide or leather. Some used sharp stone heads for chopping and cutting, also as weapons. Some tomahawks used a heavy rounded stone head for fighting instead of sharp stone heads.)

tra·vois \tra-vois\ (a type of sled formerly used by North American Indians to carry goods, consisting of two joined poles dragged by a horse or dog – see šunónkonpa)

tu·šu·he·yun·pi \ṫu-šú-he-yuŋ-pi\ (a travois, a drag, i.e. tent or tipi poles tied together to pack things on)

un·hce·la ka·ga·pi \uŋ-ḣcé-la ḳà-ġa-pi\ (the feather disk attached to the back of a dancer, so called because of the central part appears like a cactus; a dance bustle)

wa·a·ša·pe \wa-á-ša-ṗe\ (dirty or soiled hands)

wa·chi·wi \wa-chi-wi\ (dancing girl)

wa·cin·hin \wá-ciŋ-hiŋ\ (the headdress of a Dakota man, anything standing up on the head, e.g. feathers, down or soft feathers, etc.)

wa·cin·hin sa·psa·pa \wá-ciŋ-hiŋ sa-psà-pa\ (black plumes)

wa·cin·hin·ya \wá-ciŋ-hiŋ-ya\ (to use for a plume)

wa·ci·pi \wa-cí-ṗi\ (dancing, a dance)

wa·gli·hpa \wa-gli-ḣṗá\ (to fall down, i.e. once)

wa·hin·kpe \wa-híŋ-kṗe\ (arrow)

wa·h·un·un·pa \wa-h-un-un-pa\ (man in a sacred language)

wa·ḣtin·yan \wa-ḣtíŋ-yaŋ\ (to be fond of, to care for or about, to love, as in expressing love of any members of the family)

wa·kan \wa-ḳáŋ\ (sacred, holy, consecrated, incomprehensible, special, possessing or capable of giving)

wa·kan'·e·con·pila \wa-káŋ-e-coŋ-ṗi-la\ (magic, tricks of jugglery)

Wa·kan·tan·ka \Wa-ḳáŋ-taŋ-ḳa\ (the Great Spirit, The Creator, God)

wa·kan wa·ci·pi \wa-káŋ wa-cì-pi\ (a sacred dance)

wa·kan·yan \wa-káŋ-yaŋ\ (in a sacred, holy, or wonderful, or even a mysterious way)

wa·kan·yu·za \wa-káŋ-yu-za\ (to take a wife)

wa·ki·hi·ye·ce \wa-kí-hi-ye-ce\ (parents)

wa·kin·yan \wa-kíŋ-yaŋ\ (the thunderbird, so titled for the natural world of space the bird shares with thunder and lightning)

wa·ki·pu·skil iyeya \wa-kí-pu-skil iyeya\ (to make join suddenly together)

wa·ki·ta \wá-ki-ta\ (to look out for, to watch)

wak'inpi \wak'íŋpi\ (a pack)

wa·le·ga \wa-lé-ġa\ (the bladder)

wa·le·ga mi·ni·ya·ye \wa-lé-ġa min-i-ya-ye\ (a water jug)

wa·na·p'in·ki·ca·ton \wa-ná-ap'in-ki-ca-toŋ\ (to put on as a piece of neckwear, to cause to wear as a necklace)

wa·na·gi·ya·ta \wa-ná-ġi-ya-ta\ (in the land of spirits)

wan·bli·gle·ška \wan-bli-gle-ška\ (spotted eagle)

wan·hi \waŋ-hí\ (flint – a hard rock used to make sparks, by striking it against another flint rock and used to start a fire or make arrow heads and spear heads)

Wa·ni·ki·ye \Wa-ní-ki-ye\ (the Savior, i.e. Jesus Christ of Nazareth in Israel)

wa·ni·ye·tu \wa-ní-ye-tu\ (winter; a year)

wan·ju \wáŋ-ju\ (an arrow pouch – in Lakota dialect, i.e. a 'quiver' in English language)

wan·tan·ye·ya \waŋ-táe-ye-ya\ (be skillful in shooting)

wa·on·ze \wa-óŋ-ze\ (a nickname for a sakehanska, the grizzly bear)

wa·o·we·ši·ca \wa-ó-we-ši-ca\ (a bear, in general)

wa·pa·ha hetonpi \wa-pá-ha he-tòn-pi\ (a horned headdress)

wa·pe·to·ke·ca \wá-ṗe-to-k̇e-ca\ (a sign, a mark, a boundary)

wa·ši·cun \wa-ší-cuŋ\ (the white man, as used disparagingly)

Wašín \wa-šíŋ\ (fat not dried out) **Wakpá** \wa-k̇pá\ (a river) (South Platte River – English language)

waš'in \waš'in\ (bull frog)

wa·to·gya \wató-gya\ (to spoil, ruin; to take vengeance, retaliate, to kill)

wa·wa·kan·kan \wa-wá-kaŋ-kaŋ\ (one who does wonderful things)

wa·wa·ša·gya \wa-wá-ša-gya\ (to render worthless)

wa·ya·hlo·ka \wa-yá-ḣlo-ka\ (to persuade, make an impression talking)

wa·ya·ka \wa-yá-k̇a\ (a captive taken in war, a prisoner)

wi \wi\ (the sun or the moon; a month; a personification of the most immense power in creation, for it determines all seasons)

wi·ca·hpi \wi-cá-ḣpi\ (star)

wi·ca·ša \wi-cá-ša\ (man, a man, mankind)

wi·ca·t'e \wí-ca-t'e\ (an instrument with which to kill – Lakota dialect – hatchet or club – English language)

wig·wam \wig-wam\ (wigwam a small cone-shaped house)

wi·hi·ya·la \wí-hi-ya-la\ (the passing sun, the measure of clock time, the hour of the day)

wi·ma·ca \wi-ma-ca\ (a man, a male of the human species)

wi·no·na \wi-no-na\ (first born daughter)

win·yan·cin \wíṇ-yan-ciṇ\ (to buy a wife)

wi·pe·ya \wí-ṗe-ya\ (to sell a woman or girl in marriage, as once was done)

wi·sma·hin \wi-smá-hiṇ\ (an arrowhead)

Wi·wan·yank Wa·ci·pi \Wi-wáṇ-yank- Wa-cì-ṗi\ (the Sundance, a Dakota and Lakota tribal celebration of endurance in behalf of relatives or friends)

wi·ya·ta·pi·ka wacipi \wi-yá-ṫa ṗi-ḳa wa-cí-ṗi\ (a single women's dance, one performed by single young women only, and two young men do the drumming and singing)

wi·yo·hi·yan·pa \wi-yó-hi-yaṇ-ṗa\ (the east, rising sun)

wo·hle·pe s'e \wo-ḣlé-ṗe s'e\ (standing upright)

wo·on·ši·la \wó-oṇ-ši-la\ (mercy)

wo·wa·š'a·ke \wó-wa-š'a-ḳe \(strength)

wo·wi·tan·wa·ya \wō'-wi-ṫan·wa·ya\ (to glory in)

Xapáaliia (Baaxpeé which means "power transcending the ordinary." The physical manifestation of Baaxpeé is Xapáaliia, often referred to as 'medicine', which represents and acts as a conduit of Baaxpeé given to a Crow by God. – Crow dialect – Wikipedia).

yu·a·ja·ja \yu-á-ja-ja\ (to explain, to make clear e.g. a doctrine)

yu·go \yu-ġó\ (to be fatigued)

yu·o·ni·han \yu-ó-ni-haŋ\ (to honor, treat with attention)

yu·o·ni·han·yan \yu-ō'-ni-haŋ-yaŋ\ (honoring, treating politely)

yu·tke·ya \yu-tké-ya\ (deeply, as said of a bluff shore where the water is deep)

zi·ca·ho·ta \zi-cá-ho-ta\ (the common gray squirrel)

zon·ta \zóŋ-ta\ (honest, trustworthy)

zu·ya \zu-yá\ (to go out with a war party, to lead out a war party)

Made in the USA
Middletown, DE
23 June 2020